Rabbit

A Southern Summer

Love all things Southern
Buddy Hogg

William Hogg

ISBN: 978-1945190353

Edited by Ellie Locket

V2-11

Visit the website: **www.TheRabbitBook.com**

Intellect Publishing, LLC
6581 County Road 32, Suite 1195
Point Clear, AL 36564
www.IntellectPublishing.com
Inquiries to: info@IntellectPublishing.com

Acknowledgements

Like anyone trying to write, there are people and events that make your life and work better. My life was made better when I lost my job in 2003. That loss was an inspiration for me to write a letter to the editor of a local newspaper. The short version is my comments on losing a job was really not a big deal when compared to tragic circumstances surrounding others. Three different people commented to the newspaper that reading my letter encouraged them to not commit suicide. Perhaps shallow, but it also caused me to believe that there could be power in my words. That story was eventually accepted into one of the 'Chicken Soup for the Soul', series. Wow, I could even be paid for my words!

I wrote more and joined a writer's group in Rocky Mount, North Carolina and a blog site called Fanstory. Many people read my work and for the most part, feedback was positive. Every writer 'glows' from positive feedback and I had my glowing moments. The really neat thing though was that some wasn't positive, but more important, helpful. People were interested in my work and were willing to help me become better.

A breakthrough moment was moving to Fairhope, Alabama. Two years ago, I joined the Fairhope Writer's Forum. This is a dedicated group of writers, certainly more talented than me. Their feedback, encouragement and hand-holding made me tighten my work and strive to improve each time I sat behind my computer, (which is more and more these days!).

Another important venue in Fairhope is another writer's group called Pensters. This group sponsors sharing sessions with various authors. Each session caused Ah-ha moments. Professional authors striving to convey their wisdom and insight to help you become better! What a joy.

I would like to thank my publisher, Intellect Publishing and John O'Melveny Woods, for seeing value in my work and encouraging me to go that next step in writing—a novel. It's been a labor of love.

My wife, Valerie, has been an inspiration to me in so many ways. She has always been my biggest fan and supporter. That means so much. When I'm in my office writing and re-writing, she makes sure that I'm not disturbed. In fact, if I slack off and don't write for a few days...

Table of Contents

Preface

I grew up as a military brat, so early life was defined by frequent travel. What might seem an easy question to most, “Where are you from?” was not so for me. For some, the answer is based on where you were born. Doesn't work. I was born in an Army hospital in Fukuoka, Japan. For many, the answer might be as simple as you're from wherever you currently reside. I suppose that works.

Two years ago, I was asked this question at a party. I was stumbling over the answer when I realized the true answer for me. There is one place that always grabs my heart, a place that when I visit brings a sense of calm over me. The place is Troup County, Georgia. As I lay in bed that night, my mind raced back almost sixty years ago to a special summer in 1960. It was the inspiration for this book.

This book is fiction. What else could it be? I've killed a bunch of brain cells over the last sixty years, so can't remember every event and every conversation. Saying that, I can tell you that the characters and settings are real. A main character was my best friend, Virgil Gates, universally known as Virge. I suppose a strange friendship as Virge was eighty-eight when I first met him and ninety during that summer. My brother is another character, as close to an antagonist as you'll find in this book. He's certainly real and now resides in Pullman Washington. I love him today but wasn't so sure back then.

I learned a lot that summer, much of which came from Virge. Here are some “Virgeisms”, that are with me to this day.

A man who hits a woman ain't much of a man

You can treat a bee sting with chewing tobacco

When you laughin' with friends, it's hard to stay mad

Don't never close your eyes and open your mouth

Laws is laws...They ain't gotta make sense. You can't own people and you can't marry your first cousin

You can't hate your brother, no matter how aggravating he might be

If you ain't got family, you ain't got much

Family is more than your mama, daddy and close relatives. It also is people who love you and you love back

The way with chickens might be bad, but the way with men can be worse

Try your best and if it don't work out, don't fret on it. Just smile and gets on with your life

When I'm gone from this world, don't worry about me or be sad, just think about all the good times we had

When them worms get to ol' Virge, don't worry. They plantin' me a long way from the tomato plants. Ha Ha Ha

I hope you read this book and smile. I grinned every time I sat down at my computer to write it. Of course, sometimes there were tears.

Great times, great memories!

Bill

Rabbit

A Southern Summer

Chapter 1

The Beginning

It was summer of 1960. I would turn nine in June. Earlier in March, we learned Mom's pooched out belly wasn't weird. She was pregnant. There were already three of us children. My older brother's name was John Jackson Hardy. Since his first and second name started with the same letter, we called him JJ. Named after my dad and great grandpa, he was the third. I once told Mom, rather than nick-name him JJ, I would just call him the turd. He was ten. My younger brother's name was Robert, but from the day he was born, we all called him Bubba. He was seven. My name is William, but for reasons I'll fill you in on later, I was called Rabbit.

Our house was a tiny frame house in the middle of the country, so finding a private spot to speak was hard. I remember overhearing Mom's conversation with Dad. "The baby is due in August and there's no way I can have this baby with both JJ and Rabbit around at the same time. They fight like two alley cats thrown into a closet. I can handle Bubba, but not those two. We have to get them out of the house."

This scared me. Two nights ago, we huddled together in the living room and watched the movie, "Boys Town" on our black and white television. It looked to me like Father Flannigan would inherit two more boys, JJ and me. Panic turned to joy as I heard her go on to say, "I've talked to your mom and she will take Rabbit for the entire summer. My mom will take JJ. The pregnancy won't be easy at my age, but with those two boys separated with their grandparents, it should work out just fine."

Yes! This was great news. I stayed with my grandmother some each summer, usually for two or three weeks. The prospect for the entire summer was just too much. Don't get me wrong. I loved my mom and dad and our own house, but my grandmother's place was special. It was a working farm with cows, chickens, horses, gardens, and two ornery mules. There was a pond and creek for fishing and swimming. It was also where my best friend lived. His name was Virge Gates.

Some might have thought this a strange friendship. Virge was a ninety-year-old black man. He lived in an old weathered wood cabin on the property. He did work for my grandparents for free rent and pocket money. He would cut wood, take care of the yard, and general chores. His most important job involved the mules. He once described his primary job as, "I'm the mule engineer." Perhaps this was in reference to my grandfather who was a part-time farmer, but a full-time railroad engineer.

The two mules paid little attention to anyone other than Virge. They were big old mules, one named Blue and the other Buck. My grandfather could plow with them but they played with him. They would act up, pull sideways, buck against their brace and generally make a mess of things. Grandpa claimed the mules saved their sloppy behavior for when he was behind them. His rows looked squiggly. Virge's would be straight as an arrow. For some reason, those mules loved Virge. A special treat to me was when he would swing me up on their backs as they moved from their pens to the fields.

A book Grandma often read to me was Joel Chandler Harris's 'Uncle Remus and Br'er Rabbit.' My favorite story concerned the Tar Baby. Br'er Fox came up with a plan to capture Br'er Rabbit. He'd been trying to catch the old rabbit for years and when Br'er Rabbit got stuck on the tar baby, the fox wanted to punish him in special ways. Br'er Rabbit cried out, "Do what you want to me, but please, please don't throw me into that briar patch. Of course, he did, to the Rabbit's delight.

Yep, going to stay with my grandmother for the entire summer was something to look forward to. I was being thrown into the briar patch and loved it.

On the third of June, we piled into the 1959 Buick Roadmaster for the trip from Eufaula in East Alabama to LaGrange, Georgia. Bubba was left with a neighbor, so it was Mom and Dad up front. JJ behind the driver, me on the other side. Between JJ and me, was our bird-dog, Pat.

Pat was laying down, her head on my lap. Of course, the other end was pointed toward JJ. Pat was a funny dog. She loved me, and pretty much ignored JJ, so much so, it seemed like she didn't know he was there. Something else funny about her was she could smile. Her mouth would stretch upward from side to side and she'd show her teeth.

All of a sudden, JJ blurted, “Oh God, Pat pooted!” She was known to do that, and her silent seepers could make your eyes water.

As Mom rolled down her window she corrected JJ. “Don't you take the Lord's name in vain. Pat's just a dog. I'm sure it was an accident.”

“Well, I don't think so. Looks to me like she done it on purpose.”

Mom blurted out, “What in the world would make you say that?”

“Just look at her. She's got that goofy smile from ear to ear.”

I looked over at Pat. She was smiling.

“Can't you two boys just take a nap or something? It'll make the trip seem faster.”

I didn't need much encouragement. For me, the sound of tires on an old country road was a magic sleeping potion. The small stones embedded in the black surface made the tires hum with a soft *bump-de-bump-de-bump* sound. As I neared sleep, I started thinking how I first met my friend, Virge Gates.

#

It was summer of 1958. Our family was back from six years in Japan. The Air Force gave Dad most of the summer off between assignments. We stayed where my father grew up, the old home place in West-Central Georgia. My grandmother and grandfather lived there now, but there were pictures in the living room of my great-great grandmother in the front yard.

It was late June and hot. I was looking up the dirt road and had to rub my eyes. There appeared to be two people walking right on top of each other on what looked like water. The air around this weird sight was shimmering and wavy. It was a simple mirage created by mid-day heat on the road bed, but for a six-year-old boy, pure magic.

"Grandma--somethin' strange is a walkin' down the road."

She put her ice tea down, smoothed her gingham summer frock, and with her hand shielding her eyes took a look. "Bill, that's nothing strange, it's just old Virge come down to help your Grandpa put the mules in the harness. They're going to plow up some of the new ground."

I looked again. The heat shimmer disappeared as he got closer, and I could tell it was an old black man. He was not a large man, just tall and slim. There were crinkles around his large, brown, expressive eyes. His teeth, when smiling, looked like the keys on my grandma's piano. He was dressed pretty much the same way as I always saw him from that day on. On the top of his head was a sweat stained railroad engineer's cap. He had on a pair of blue denim overalls, and a long sleeve cotton shirt. On his feet were scuffed, brown leather brogans.

Virge walked in a way I'd never seen. It's like he would plant one foot in front of himself and then glide forward the rest of his body to catch up with his foot. My grandma saw me once trying to copy his walk. She just laughed, saying, "You ain't got it in you to walk like that."

Virge tipped his hat to my grandma as he said, "Hey Ms. Louise. I'm here to help Mr. Horace with them mules. Who's the little tow head boy on the rocker?"

"Hey Virge--thanks for coming. That there's Mr. Jack's middle boy, Bill. His brothers JJ and Bubba are around somewhere. Bill, this is Virge Gates. How about taking him out back. Your grandpa is waiting for him."

For the first and last time, Virge addressed me in the way so common in the South those days. "Mister Bill, how old you be?"

It surprised me to be called Mister, but I'd been taught on how to address older people, so I said, "Mr. Gates, I'm six and nine-eighths. You don't have to call me Mr., just Bill or Billy. That's what everybody calls me." He continued the Mr. and Miss connection with most of my family. He did call Bubba just plain old Bubba. According to Virge, Mr. and Bubba just didn't go together. Me though, he treated special. He called me Rabbit.

He also asked me not to call him Mr. "You do that, and I be lookin' aroun' to see who you talkin' to. You just call me Virge."

My grandma once asked Virge why he called me Rabbit. "Cuz he's like the rabbit. He sits still and quiet, but all the time, he's pointin' dem ears and movin' dem eyes. He takin' it all in. Ain't nobody gonna get one by the rabbit!" For whatever reason, it stuck. Everybody started calling me Rabbit. I didn't mind.

JJ and I fought all the time, and Bubba was just a baby. By default, Virge became my best friend. I asked my father once how old Virge was. His answer said it all. "I'm not sure, but Virge was an old man when I was your age." I later found out he was eighty-eight.

That summer and any time we would visit, I would hang out with Virge. I would help him do his chores and he would help me do mine. If we were done, we would go fishing or just sit on his front porch and rock. He was often visited by his niece, Carrie and her son, Joe Leslie.

They became part of my life too.

Chapter 2

The Watermelon

Waking up was automatic. We've driven to my grandma's house a zillion times. Her house is on a dirt-road cut off from the main highway. The sound of the car leaving the country road and onto the dirt road was distinctive. I always got a catch in my throat at the turn. With my dad in the military, it could be difficult to tell people where your home was. It was easy for me. Home was right here.

From the turn, it was about one-half mile to the old home place. We stopped in front of the house. It looked the same as before, painted white with a wide columned front porch. Tall oak and magnolia trees draped the front and side, providing cooling shade on the porch. Standing in the front portico was my grandmother. She was dressed as usual in a cotton, gingham, long dress. Grandma even worked in the garden with a dress. I never saw her in pants.

Mom got out and opened the door for me. Pat jumped out of the car and ran to hang out with a mongrel dog name Skippy. JJ got out and threw rocks at a jay bird. Dad got my bag out of the trunk. Walking to the side of the car, he stuck his hand out to me. “Okay, buddy. We're going to leave you here with Grandma. I want you to promise to be a good boy and help out around the farm. You've got your grandma, grandpa, Virge and Skippy, so you shouldn't be too lonely.”

Mom gave me a big hug. "Rabbit, you know I'm going to have another baby. It's going to be real busy at home getting ready for it and everything. It will sure be lonely without you. Are you sure you'll be okay with your grandma and grandpa for the entire summer?"

Giving an obligatory sniffle, I replied, "Yes Ma'am. I reckon I'll be just fine." She and my dad walked slowly toward the car. Calling for Pat and JJ, they packed into the Buick . Mom took a quick peek back. My grandma had her arm around my shoulder. Mom and Dad waved. I waved back. I'm sure Mom thought I was sad

I guess Grandma thought I was sad too, so she made one of my favorite dinners. My plate was filled with chicken fried steak, fresh sliced tomatoes, green beans, fried okra and rice topped with white milk gravy. I'd mention the buttermilk biscuits, but they weren't special. I pretty much got them every day.

After dinner, we sat on the front porch and rocked. I wanted to run up to Virge's cabin, but thought it best to wait. Grandma told me he was going to be down first thing in the morning to work on her front fence.

I was anxious to see Virge, but my Grandpa had me all excited about the evening. He asked me if I wanted to stay up and listen to the radio and the heavyweight boxing championship of the world.

As a younger man, my grandpa boxed as an amateur. He had an old cigar box, slap full of clippings. He did pretty well as a welterweight. He boxed in local textile leagues and state tournaments. Because of him, I followed boxing through the sports pages of the newspapers. I was thrilled to stay up and listen. The fight was between an American, Floyd Patterson and a Swede, Ingmar Johansson.

We settled in and munched on popcorn. I was drinking my iced tea and remember asking my grandfather how come his tea was in such a small glass and didn't have any ice in it. The boxing match started and it was very exciting. Both fighters were down on the canvas a couple of times and then Patterson seemed to be getting the best of Johansson. To me, it was pretty much a "black and white" thing. I wanted Patterson to win because he was an American, while Johansson was from Sweden. Well, it was a "black and white" issue for my grandpa too. He wanted Johansson to win because he was white and Patterson black.

In the sixth round, Patterson knocked Johansson down and out. My grandpa leaped out of his chair and ripping the radio from the table, hurled it through the window. The only sound after the shattered glass was my grandpa muttering, "Oh Shit!" Reaching through the window to retrieve the radio, he sliced his arm open on a shard of glass hanging from the sill. I woke Grandma up and she wrapped a towel around his arm and cinched it tight with a belt. They got into their pick-up truck and drove into town to get Grandpa fixed up

This actually made an article in the local newspaper the next day. The headline while not complete, told much of the story. "Heavyweight fight in Sweden sends local man to emergency room."

I got to see Virge after all. He came down to sit with me while they went to the hospital. First, he showed me where in the garage, extra panes of glass had already been cut and stored. Back inside, I swept up the glass and Virge replaced the window panes. Like in many of his tasks, he patiently showed me how to caulk and replace glass.

By the time I went to bed, I was tired but excited. This was my first day and the adventures had already begun

Grandma let me sleep in a little bit. Of course, sleeping in has a whole new meaning in the rural South. It meant she let me sleep past sun-up. I was up by seven, had breakfast, gathered the eggs and then joined Virge for one of his chores.

If you're going to be doing outside work in west central Georgia in June, you best get an early start. Virge had been working for an hour when I got there at eight. The job today was pulling honeysuckle and jasmine vines away from Grandma's front fence.

The previous summer, I was given a little mongrel dog we named Skippy. Today, he was supervising. He would interrupt his nap under the shade of a magnolia tree, look up and check on us from time to time.

Skippy jumped up and started barking. Virge and I stopped working to see what got his attention. Old-man Caruth was walking up the road toward us. You could tell it was him, because he walked kinda gimpy. As my grandpa used to say, he had a hitch in his giddy-up. He was a tall, gangly, white man, always dirty and smelly, with a smile like a picket fence; some white teeth, but lots of gaps. Folks used to say old man Caruth was good for nothing. I'm here to tell you that ain't exactly so. He could sure raise watermelons.

He stopped at the front yard. Skippy wandered over and sniffed his leg. With that done, he lifted his leg high and peed on his pants. Old man Caruth kicked out at him, yelling, "You dumb damn dog!" I took a look at Virge for a sign, and didn't see even a glimmer of a smile. I said nothing. I always thought Skippy was pretty smart, though my grandma did usually refer to him as that damn dog.

"Howdy Rabbit. Is your grandpa home?"

"No, sir, he ain't. He and Grandma drove into town to sell some eggs at the farmers' market."

"Well, don't matter. I'm glad to see old Virge here anyhow. Virge, do you know any young nigras that'll come pick my watermelons? I pay five cents apiece if they pick em and load em in the truck."

Virge waited a few seconds like he was thinking it over, and then replied, "No, Sa', can't say as I do. I'd do it myself, but I'm ninety-years-old."

"Well, Virge, if you think of somebody, jes' let me know. Rabbit, since you a neighbor and all, you can come down, pick whatever melon you want for twenty-five cents." With a scowl at Skippy and spitting tobacco juice his way, old man Caruth headed out. Skippy walked over to where his pee had dripped of old man Caruth's britches. He proceeded to pee again. People claim dogs are just animals and basically dumb. There was more than just a dumb dog look on his face. It all but announced, "Dumb damn human."

I waited until old-man Caruth got down the road some, and turning to Virge, I asked, "Didn't you just tell me Sugar Butts and Joe Leslie were lookin' for some work?" They were his niece and grand-nephew, the nickname for her was his, not mine. It came from the fact that even though she was all normal up top, she had about the biggest butt you'd ever see on a person. Her real name was Miss Carrie.

"Yes, I said that, but I wouldn't have nobody I know work for dat nasty ol' man. Anyhow, most folks pay ten cents apiece, not five. I just don't cotton to dat man. He's what most folks call white trash. Next time you see his wife, take a look at her face. She'll powder it up some, but you'll still see the bruises where he be hittin' on her. You know old Virge likes to preach and teach, so here comes one. Any man who hits a woman, ain't much of a man. Plus, even though it was before I was born, his granddaddy or someone in his line, used to own my mama."

I tried to understand what he just said. "Virge, do you mean he owed your mama, like money or somethin'?"

"Naw Rabbit, I mean one of his kinfolk used to own my mama. It be like your grandpa ownin' them two mules, or his pick-up truck. My mama was a slave.

"Virge, I'm pretty young, but I know you can't own somebody!"

"Well Rabbit, you is right, but long time ago, you could. Right here where we standin', used to be all sorts of 'owned' people, working this here farm. They used to grow cotton and the owner used to have slaves to do all the work. Ol' man Caruth's family used to own his bottom land and the land across the highway from this place. Look across the pasture.

All them terraces used to be part of a cotton field. Them ol' rock piles are where they picked them out of the field and throwed them out of the way."

For an eight-year-old kid, this was just plain strange. Looking at Virge, perhaps in a different way, I said, "I want one of them watermelons."

"Okay Rabbit, when we get done here, we'll walk on down and get us a melon. We can put it in the spring house and let it get nice and cool. Come this evenin', it'll be good to eat."

"Virge - I don't want to buy one. I want to steal one."

"Hey, Rabbit, if you ain't got the money, I'll give you the quarter."

"It ain't the money. I got a quarter. It just seems we ought to steal it."

Virge looked at me with a puzzled look. He eventually countered, "You been to church with me and Sugar Butts, and you know the Bible say, 'Thou Shalt Not Steal'. You remember dat?"

"Yeah--I reckon I do, but don't it say something about Thou Shalt Not Own Somebody."

Virge chuckled as he said, "Naw, it don't say nothin' bout dat. In fact, them Jews got traded back and forth to all sorts of people and they was slaves themselves."

"I still say we ought to steal a watermelon."

"Rabbit, dat ain't a good idea."

"Look now, if we wait until 7:30 tonight, it ought to be dark enough so nobody sees us. What do you think?

"Yeah, that oughta be about right."

At 7:15 I told my grandma I was going to walk down to the lake and catch a big ol' bass. I just hoped she didn't go. I met Virge and off we went to old man Caruth's watermelon patch. We got there and waited for a few minutes. We were about 100 yards away. The porch light was off and there was nobody on the back porch, so we snuck over the barbed wire fence and out into the watermelons. Virge found us a good one, and cut it off the vine with his Barlow knife.

If there ever was a dumb old damn dog, it was old man Caruth's coon dog. It began barking those crazy howls, *oooow, oooow, oooow*. The back door slammed open, and old man Caruth bolted out in his underwear with a shotgun in hand. He yelled, "I know you boys. You best put the watermelon down and get on out of here."

We got on out of there all right, but running, Virge with the watermelon under his arm. First the flash of a double barrel shotgun, and then, KABOOM, KABOOM. Had we had any logic about us, we wouldn't have worried. Given the distance and light condition, he couldn't possibly recognize us, much less hit us. There weren't no logic though, just pure wet your pants scared.

My legs were churning, and then in a panic, I remembered Virge. I stopped, turned around and looked for him. *Oh no, what happened*? Then I glanced to my left, and there he was, about ten yards ahead of me. I reckon he must have hopped the fence.

We ran for a few more minutes, and then stopped. It's hard to get your breath when you've been running, and even harder when you start laughing like a couple of schoolgirls. We caught our breath and finally walked on up to Virge's cabin. Joe Leslie and Sugar Butts were there, so we cut the watermelon right up and ate it. It had to have been the best watermelon of all time. And why not? You know what they say about forbidden fruit?

The next afternoon, my grandma told me she saw old-man Caruth at the Farmer's market that morning. "Rabbit, Mr. Caruth told me that two nigra boys stole some watermelons out of his patch last night. He said he took a shot at the two while they were running away. According to him, one was tall and lanky and one real short, almost like a midget. You haven't heard anybody talking about it have you?"

I stopped whittling away at a stick and paused. Scratching my head, I said, "No Ma'am. I ain't seen nobody this morning but Virge and Miss Carrie and they didn't mention it. According to Mr. Caruth, it couldn't be any of us. Miss Carrie can't run, Virge ain't no boy and I ain't black."

With the slightest of smiles, she said, "No, I reckon not."

Chapter 3

The Gun

Saturday mornings were special. My grandma and grandpa went to town where they'd take baby chicks, eggs, or milk to the farmer's market. Sometimes I would tag along, but they preferred me going to the movies. Since they didn't like me going by myself, they would pick up my cousin Wesley to go as well. Wesley was ten years old. I should be kind since he's my cousin, but there's no way around it. Wesley was weird. He was short, fat and had a crew-cut. Not just any kind of crew-cut, but one where his hair, right in front, was combed up and set with Brylcreem. If a little dab would do ya, I guess he thought a big old gob would do it better. His two front teeth were large and slightly gapped.

Virge and I loved nicknames. With Wesley, it was 'Beaver'. He complained to his mom, before Virge told him that the Indians thought the beaver was holy and gave your dreams great power. I don't know if that was pure bull, because Virge does know a lot of stuff. Anyhow, Wesley went along with it.

All Beaver wanted to do was talk about or ride horses. One look at him and you felt sorry for the horse. There were two horses at our farm, but I could always find better things to do than ride them.

I once asked my grandma why I couldn't go to the movies with Virge. She quit rocking and looked at me before replying, "Well, Rabbit, the theater doesn't allow nigras to sit down where you sit. They have to sit upstairs in the balcony."

"Well, that ain't no problem. I'll just sit up there with Virge."

"Honey, I don't think that would work out. Plus, your cousin Wesley really enjoys going with you."

I just rolled my eyes.

Beaver and I had our routine down pat. Grandma and Grandpa dropped us downtown and gave me two dollars. Wesley always had money of his own. In fact, he would have so much change in his pockets that he would jingle as he walked. It was embarrassing. We'd head over to Charlie Joseph's for lunch. You could get a hot dog and bag of chips for fifty cents. For a dime you could get a cola. Beaver always got cola. I'd get ice water, because I'd want that dime in the theater.

After lunch, we'd head around the block to the theater. Admission was fifty cents. A large popcorn and a cola would set you back seventy-five cents. If I felt like it, I'd lay into a bag of Raisinets or a Baby Ruth.

The movie format was pretty much the same. Usually there was an ongoing serial. At the time, we were into Flash Gordon Conquers the Universe. That would be followed by a cartoon, a news reel and then the movie, which was generally Tarzan or a Western. Sometimes, the guy who played Flash Gordon was also Tarzan.

This particular Saturday was different. The movie was great. It was called 'High Noon'. It was about a sheriff who met a lady who didn't want him shooting up people any more. It was supposed to be his last day on the job. Anyhow, some guy he sent to prison comes back to town and poor Sheriff Kane couldn't get anyone to help him. It looked like it would end with a gunfight between him and the outlaw Frank Miller.

Halfway through the movie, Beaver leaned over and whispered, "We could be home riding horses. This movie is dumb."

I just elbowed him and growled, "Shut Up." I was at the edge of my chair for the entire movie.

Other than it being a great movie, I kept thinking, *my grandpa has a gun that looks like Sheriff Kane's.*

Later that afternoon at the farm, my grandparents said that they were going to walk down to the pond and try a little fishing and did I want to go. I said, "No, I'm really tired. I'll just stay home and watch television." They should have been suspicious. I'm never too tired to fish.

They barely got out the door when I started looking for the gun. The first place I looked was the big dresser in their bedroom. The first drawer had all sorts of stuff in it. What I found wasn't what I was looking for, but was quite interesting. It was a large box of condoms. My older brother had told me all about 'rubbers', but the picture I had in my head wasn't even close. Somehow, I pictured inner-tube black rubber that had to be strapped on. The inside box cover included instructions that showed me wrong. All of them in the box were wrapped in their own little red packages. Hmm, Trojans. I put one in my pocket for later study. Now I had another mystery to solve; *who the heck did they belong to*? With the second drawer, I hit pay-dirt. Under some pajamas was a .38 caliber police special, the gun I was looking for. I once saw my grandpa use the gun to shoot a snake that crawled under the chicken house. This was not a modern looking gun. It was a big old, bulky revolver and looked much like Sheriff Kane's.

I figured my grandparents were now down by the pond, about a quarter of a mile from the home place. It seemed safe enough to pull the gun out, stick it through my belt and practice fast draw in front of the closet mirror. I thought I was getting pretty good, pulling the gun from my belt, doing a quarter turn and pretending to shoot old Frank Miller. All of a sudden, the gun went off with a loud BOOM. It punched a hole through the mirror, not through old Frank, but right about at what would have been my belly button.

I tossed the gun back in the drawer and slammed it shut. Running for all I was worth I circled back around the pond and came up behind my grandparents. They were walking real fast, so I figured they must have heard the noise. Almost out of breath, I bleated, "Did y'all hear that? It sounded like a gun shot."

All the way back to the house, I was trying to think of a story. I'm pretty good at that sort of thing. Nothing I thought of sounded believable. Standing in front of the newly shot up mirror, my grandpa asked a question with little wiggle room. "Rabbit did you take the gun out of my drawer and shoot it?"

"Yes, Sir, I did. Sheriff Kane had a gun like it in the movie this morning. I just wanted to see a real one."

"Well, Rabbit, there won't be a movie in your plans for awhile. I'm going to have to figure out some extra chores so you can pay for a new mirror."

He figured something out alright. My biggest chore had to do with chickens, feeding them and gathering eggs. Now, I had to sweep and shovel cow poop out of the milk house. It seemed fair. No one made me pull that gun out. Virge thought it real fair. The milk house was one of his chores. When he saw me there the next morning and found out what happened, he laughed and laughed.

A little irritated, I asked, “Are you going to help me?”

“Sho nuff Sheriff, Sho nuff.”

Chapter 4

Yellow Jacket War

Virge once told me, “When everything looks good, smells good, and seems good, you best look over your shoulder. You gotta' remember, God has a sense of humor.” He was right again.

I was resting on the front porch when my Grandma Nan, drove up in her 1949 Plymouth. She was my mom's mother. Out of the back seat, popped my older brother, JJ, with a small suitcase. I found out my grandparents were headed south to Florida to take care of my sick aunt's family, so JJ would be staying with us for five days.

When Grandma Nan got ready to leave, she came over and gave me a big hug. "Rabbit, I'm sure you've been lonely all by yourself. Won't it be nice to have your brother around to play with? Plus, you've got a birthday coming in a few days and I know you'll want JJ around."

Well, I bit my tongue, hugged her back and smiled.

Had you asked me, "Would you rather be hit in the head with a stick, or have your brother JJ stay with you?" I’m sure my first question would be: “Now how big is that stick?”

I decided the best thing to do was just steer clear of my brother. Lucky for me, he actually got along with Beaver. They got together a lot and rode horses, which suited me just fine. I could continue doing what I wanted.

The next morning, I hollered out to my grandma, "I got the eggs in and pulled bugs off the tomatoes. Is there anything else you want me to do?" The side to side shake of her head meant I could visit with Virge.

I walked up to his cabin, which was just a short way from their house. The cabin was of roughhewn pine and had never seen an ounce of paint. It was weathered gray, the color of a dirty dime. The shaded front porch wrapped around the front side. Inside the four-room cabin was two bedrooms, a kitchen with sitting area and a living room. It had wide-planked pine floors throughout. The cabin was surrounded by large pecan trees, so was always shady in the summer.

As I came to the cabin, I noticed Virge was placing brush in a pile up front. "Hey, Virge, whatcha' doin?"

"Hey yourself. I'm just cleaning up a bit. I'm goin' to move these old sticks and sweep up all them leaves. You come to help ol Virge?"

"Sure--I'll help." Virge and I had a great work relationship. We helped each other do work or chores, or the two of us would go fishing, or swimming in the creek. Sometimes we would just sit on his front porch and talk.

I picked up a branch and dragged it over to the burn pile. All of a sudden, the air around me was swirling with hundreds of buzzing bees. In the process of moving the branch, I had upset a large yellow jacket nest. They swarmed all around me. About five had already stung me on my arm. I near scared Virge to death, because I was doing a little dance and yelling, "Damn, damn, damn!" Virge came running over. He was swatting at me with a towel he had pulled off a line. Lifting me at the waist, he scooted me out of the area. Setting me down, he was still beating the yellow jackets away with his towel.

"Are you all right?"

I know Virge got stung real bad his own self, but there he was, checking on me. "Yeah, I reckon, but my arm feels like a bunch of people pinched the devil out of me."

"Let me look at it." Virge pulled the sleeve back. The long sleeve cotton shirt I wore didn't prevent the stings, but slowed them down. "Rabbit, them jackets popped you pretty good. You got five or six whelps on your arm. I know it hurts, cuz I got me some too. Your brother JJ would probably be cryin' and hollerin'. How come you ain't?"

"They stung you too, and you ain't crying. Plus, when I was a little boy, I decided it didn't make much sense to cry about things that hurt you on the outside. It just don't do no good. You know JJ and I fight all the time, and it bothers him when he hurts me and I don't cry."

Virge looked at me a little puzzled and asked, "You mean you don't never cry?"

"No, I mean I just don't cry when things hurt me on the outside. Those jackets stung me, but crying won't make the hurt go away. Do you remember when you helped me bury my dog Skippy last week?"

Virge looked at me and replied, "Yeah, I do. It was a sad thing. Skippy was a good ol dog."

"Well, I cried when it happened, because it hurt me on the inside. Come to think of it, you cried too, so burying Skippy maybe hurt you on the inside."

"Naw, Rabbit, I wasn't cryin'. When I was shovelin' that hole, some of that old red dirt blowed in my eyes... I do know some things to make your arm feel better. The first thing is we got to put on some chewin' tobacco."

Virge put a wad of tobacco in a tin can and poured some baking soda on it. Then adding some well water, he smushed it up with the handle end of a hammer. He was telling me this was what his daddy did for him. When he had mashed it up real good, he spread it over my arm and wrapped a wet towel around it. Maybe it was the constant talk, or a miracle cure, all I know is the pain went away.

After a while, Virge spoke up, "The other thing that'll help the pain is we get back at them durn jackets."

"How we gonna do that?"

With a sly smile Virge responded, "Yellow Jacket nests always have two holes. One's like the front door they comes in and the other's like the back door where they leaves. We find the holes in the ground, and we cover up the back hole with one of them barrel tops. Then we pour us some gasoline down the other hole. We cover the hole up with the other barrel top. The jackets breathe all dat stuff and they die. Old Virge has done this a million times. It always works."

Virge knew a lot of outdoor stuff. I figured his plan would work. We went to his small storage shed and pulled out the gas can. After locating the escape hole, Virge put the barrel top over it and told me to stand on it. He then went over to the other hole, quickly poured gas down it and covered it with the other barrel top and stood on it.

The plan was well underway when my brother JJ walked over. I love my brother now, but not so much in those days. In fact, he was a bully and a royal pain in the ass. He approached, took a look and asked, "What y'all doing?"

Virge told him about our plan. JJ listened, and looking at Virge, popped off, "You ain't going to kill the yellow jackets your way. We need to dump some more gas in the hole. Then we need to dump some kerosene over there where Rabbit is standin'. The two will create a chemical reaction and kill them all."

Virge rolled his eyes and looked at JJ with irritation. "I don't know about no chemical reaction, but I'm 90 years old and done killed lots of yellow jackets. I'm sayin', we don't have to do more'n we've done."

JJ, never short on cocky, started pouring more gas down the hole. He then walked over to the shed and got the kerosene, which he poured down the hole I was standing on. It should have been a hint. Already, it was obvious the yellow jackets were most likely dead, because there weren't any buzzing around out of either hole. He then covered the hole back up and told me to stand on the barrel top. He walked over to the hole near Virge, took a match out of his pocket, lit it and threw it in the hole. He then put the barrel top back on the hole and stood on it. Yelling at me, "Rabbit, take your barrel top off the hole."

I did, and nothing happened right away. All of a sudden, the ground swelled up a little and there was a sound, like, WHUMP. Flame whipped back through the hole in front of me, but there was an explosion under the barrel top that JJ stood on. The top lifted off the ground about an inch. The force must have gone plumb through the barrel top and into JJ's bare feet. He jumped off the top and started yelling, "Ow, ow, ow, ow,ow,ow," lifting one foot and then the other, hopping around like crazy. Virge later told me that he hoped it didn't rain for forty days and nights, because JJ did one heck of an Indian rain dance except he should have been yelling, "Woo, woo, woo, woo, woo, woo, woo."

Once we decided JJ wasn't seriously hurt, Virge and I started laughing. He made me laugh even harder when he sat on the ground, grabbed his knees and rocked back and forth. JJ ran away. I knew for certain I had a beating coming. I didn't care. It was worth it.

With tears in my eyes, I looked over at Virge and said,

"Hey Virge, I cry when I laugh hard too."

Virge whooped in air to catch his breath before saying, "Me too, Rabbit, me too!"

Chapter 5

A Bird in the Hand

Yesterday, I was eight, but not today. It's my birthday and I'm nine.

I should be up, but found myself lying in bed, looking at the way the sun came through the window. Grandma has an old house, so dust is everywhere, even in the air. The light coming through the window struck the dust and made the air shimmer with sparkles of color. It was a great day to just lie there.

Grandma yelled up the stairs, "Rabbit, are you up?"

"Yes Ma'am," I replied. It wasn't really a lie. I'm awake, so I'm up.

"Well, hurry on downstairs. I want you to see your Grandpa before he goes off to the station."

I picked up my clothes from the floor and put them back on. I'd only worn them for two days, so figured they'd be fine. I did turn my underpants inside-out before putting them on.

I traipsed down the narrow stairs and straight for the bathroom. My grandparents were in the kitchen drinking coffee, but there was immediate business for me to take care of.

Leaving the bathroom, I went to the kitchen. It was the hub of the house. Unless company came, we always ate there instead of the dining room. After supper my grandma and grandpa would sit there and talk or play gin rummy or cribbage. I walked in and plopped into my usual chair. They had already eaten, but set a small plate out for me with two sausage biscuits and a glass of milk.

Nobody was saying much until my grandpa reached behind his chair and handed me a long package. I had no idea what it was. It was about three and a half feet long and wrapped with butcher paper and string. My grandpa simply said, "Open it."

With no finesse and little care, I ripped the paper off. Inside was a Daisy No. 25, pump-action BB gun. Every kid wanted this gun. The magazine held fifty BB's, the stock and grip were wood, and it had a fixed front sight and adjustable back sight. I just held it in my hands and looked at it.

Clearing his throat, my grandpa said, "Happy birthday, Rabbit. I heard you talking to your cousin Wesley about a BB gun, so I called your dad and mom to see if it was okay to get you one. What do you think?"

Grandpa wasn't much of a hugging guy, but I got up and hugged him anyhow. "Thank you, Grandpa. This is great. Shoot, Beaver only has a Red Rider BB gun. It ain't nearly as good as this one."

"Well, I'm glad you like it. Your dad asked that you let Virge teach you how to shoot. You probably don't know this, but Virge is the one who taught his grand-nephew Joe Leslie and your daddy when they were about your age. All he's got to shoot now is his old .22 bolt-action rifle, but he's about the best shot around. He'll teach you good."

My chores for the morning were to gather eggs, pick beans and cucumbers and pull bugs off tomato plants. I finished in record time and headed up to Virge's with my new BB gun and a tube of 250 BB's.

Grandpa must have told Virge I was coming because he was ready for me. In the corner of his yard, three hay bales were stacked one on top of another. On the top bale, a white cardboard target was tied on with jute twine. With red paint, four circles were drawn from large to small. The largest circle as big around as a basketball, the smallest, central circle about the size of a silver dollar.

As he saw me approach, he smiled and said, "Hey, Rabbit. I heard you got yourself a new gun." I showed it to him with pride.

"Hoo-whee, It's a good one. Are you ready for me to teach you how to use it?"

"I'm ready, but I already read the instructions. It's got fifty BBs in it and I'm ready to shoot it."

"I'm sure you are, but I promised your grandpa that I would teach you right. The first thing you need to know is that this is called a BB gun. It ain't called no BB toy. You've already done one foolish thing."

"What, what did I do?"

"Well, the first time you showed me the gun, you pointed the business end *at me*. That's something you don't never do with a gun. That there gun could easily put an eye out. I only got two eyes, and one of them ain't doin too good. You could have put old Virge in a world of hurt."

"I'm sorry. I didn't even know I did it. I was just excited and ready to go."

"Alright, then here's lesson one and two. Never point toward something you don't want to shoot at and don't be in no big rush. Slow down and be safe. Bring it over and let's take a look."

Virge took the gun and showed me how to cock and engage the first BB. Any time he showed me something, there was always a lesson.

"When you get a little stronger, you should point the gun toward the ground to pump it. For now, I want you to get down on one knee, wedge the butt of the gun between your knee and the ground and point it straight up. You also got to watch out for your fingers. If you ain't careful that slide will pop back and pinch you bad."

Two additional hay bales placed about thirty feet from the target, would be our shooting platform. "Okay, Rabbit, since you is right handed, put that hand around the grip here. Put your left hand up on the wooden handle. Rest your arm and gun on the hay bale. Now, tilt your head to look down the rear sight and close your eye which is furthest away from the rifle, and leave the other eye open. Now center the sight at the front with the notch in back toward that target. Take a deep breath and slowly let it out. When you feel comfortable, take a shot."

It sounded easy enough. I did what he said and took my shot. Virge's response told the story. "Hey, you done pretty good; you hit the hay bales. Let me show you one time and then you try again."

Virge lined up and did exactly what he asked me to do, and took his shot. The difference was that there was a BB hole right in the center of the innermost circle.

"How did you get to be so good?"

Chuckling, Virge said, "When I was a little boy, we couldn't afford many bullets. Every time I shot, my daddy expected me to bring home a squirrel or a rabbit to eat. When you either hit what you're shootin' at or go hungry, you get pretty good."

Virge worked with me for about thirty minutes. One of his key points was how to pull on the trigger. “When you squeeze that slice of lemon in your tea, you don't just jerk it in all at one time. You squeeze it in nice and slow. Same thing with the trigger on a gun.”

After twenty minutes of instruction, I was hitting the target every time and mostly in the inner circles.

"You're doing really good. Keep practicing and you'll be a good shot like your daddy. You best be heading home for lunch. My grand-nephew, Joe Leslie, is bringing us some cans from the diner downtown. In a day or two we'll line a bunch of them up and have us a shooting contest."

The next morning after chores, I got my gun and rushed back to Virge's cabin. A splash of color caught my sight. It was the same color as the circles on the targets. A redbird landed in a Chinaberry tree right in front of me. Stopping and breathing slow, I cocked my gun. Lining up like I was shown and slowly pulling the trigger, I fired. Almost instantly, you could hear the impact. The BB striking the bird was accompanied by a small puff of red feathers. Running over and picking up the bird, I continued to Virge's.

When I arrived, Virge was sweeping off his front porch. He cheerfully greeted me, "What you in such a big hurry for?"

I opened my hand to show him the bird. "I saw this bird in the tree and I did everything like you taught me. It wasn't a big target, but I got him."

As I looked to Virge, I could see he wasn't excited. Putting down his broom, he said, "Come on over and sit next to me on the porch."

I did. Virge was silent for a moment before he said, "Put down your gun for a minute." After I did, he said, "Now, put both of your hands around that bird and close your eyes."

I thought this strange, but did what he asked. "Is the bird still warm?"

"Yes."

"With your eyes closed, can you see that bird sitting up in that tree?"

"Yes."

"What was the bird doing?"

"Not much, just flying and maybe chirping a little."

"Well, Rabbit, that bird is called a Cardinal. When they is red like that, they are the daddy bird. So that bird probably had a wife bird and this time of year, probably some baby birds. Just know, that bird ain't never going to fly again, ain't never going to chirp again and ain't never going to see his wife or babies again. You can open your eyes now and see that bird for what he is, dead."

I opened my eyes and opened my hands. My tears ran on to the dead bird. "I never thought about any of that. I was proud of my good shot and now I don't feel too good. I don't think I'll ever shoot my gun again."

“No, don't feel that way. We're both going to have a good time with that gun. Joe's coming tomorrow with a bunch of cans. Look at it dis way, you've only owned the gun two days and done already learned the three most important things about ownin' it.”

“I have?”

“Sure, what did you learn yesterday?”

“I learned to never be in a hurry with a gun, and never point it toward something I wasn't going to shoot.”

“Yep, those are good lessons, but today, you learned the most important thing of all.”

“What's that?”

“You learned that when you do point a gun toward something on purpose, you need to know what might happen once you pull that trigger. See, I ain't worried about you.

Some folks go through their whole life without learning what you know. Hand me that little bird and we'll go bury it."

Chapter 6

Shooting in Life

Virge was right. I did learn a bit about shooting my BB gun. For sure, no more bird hunting. Once my chores were done, I headed up to Virge's cabin, gun and all.

Since it was Saturday, his grand-nephew, Joe Leslie was already setting up a bunch of cans with all sorts of shooting stations. There were large commercial cans that once held tomatoes and green beans, small cans, snuff cans and sardine cans. The sardine can was the last in a long line of cans. The thin metal top was removed and tied by a length of string to the bottom of the can. It was hung up over a tree limb. Even in a light breeze, the can moved all over the place.

Unlike Virge, Joe was a large man. His shoulders were huge and his chest reminded me of the large bull in the pasture. His belly was big too. He liked to pat it and say, "I earned every flabby inch of this here belly."

Seeing me, his face lit up in a big old smile. "Happy birthday, Rabbit. I brought you two big 500 tube packages of BB's and set us up a shooting range. Come on and let me show you."

It was amazing what all he put up. He hauled additional hay bales and cut logs out and had cans stacked everywhere. The first target was a large number ten can. The label was still on it and said, cut green beans. It wasn't standing upright, but laying on its side. The shiny bottom was painted with red circles, a lot like Virge's paper targets. All three of us banged it pretty good.

The next setup was amazing. Joe had laid out a series of cans, small ones to each side, working into a middle standing upright, with a snuff can on top. On each side of the middle can, were two larger cans set on end. The layout looked kind of like a boat.

"What's that supposed to be, Joe?"

"That there is the German Battleship, Bismark. There's a movie out right now called, 'Sink the Bismark'. We're going to be the British Navy and try and sink it. Our first shot is going to be like this." Joe took a shot from the hip, not even aiming. He hit one of the cans.

"See, just like those British guys that fired on it. They hit it lots of times, but it was going to take the perfect shot to sink the big old ship. To do that, you gotta take aim and shoot the little snuff can in the middle. Here, you try."

I took my first shot from the hip and hit one of the large cans in the middle. Now, taking my time and aiming at the small snuff can, I shot again. Well, the old boat was still floating. Lucky for the British, Virge followed me and sunk it. We had a great time with our contest. Joe and Virge were better than me, but I was actually pretty close. The last station with the sardine can was something else.

The small sardine can was pretty far away and moving all over the place in the slight wind. It was Virge's turn and he took his shot. He missed! He kind of went, "Hummph", and handed the gun to Joe. He rested his gun across some hay bales and slowly took his shot and was rewarded with a loud ping.

"Okay, Rabbit, it's your turn. Let me help you a little on this one. Lay your gun across the bales but just watch the can for a minute. Tell me what you see."

"The can is moving, mostly from the left to the right."

"Okay, the key to a shot like this is to shoot to where the can is going to be, not where it is. Got it?"

"Yep." I slowly exhaled and squeezed the trigger. Ping. I looked over to Joe and Virge, both were smiling. I didn't gloat or anything, but it did feel pretty good to do better than Virge.

Virge said, "Okay, you boys done good. I'm going to go in, chip up some ice and bring out some lemonade. Why don't you two just sit up on the porch for a spell." We did just that, selecting two rocking chairs in the shade.

"Thank you, Joe, for setting up all those cans and bringing the BB's. That was a lot of fun."

"My pleasure. You shot good, especially that last can. That's not an easy shot."

"Your advice helped."

"Talking about advice, does the old man fill your ears with it?"

"Yeah, but it is all good. I may not always follow it, but I do listen."

"Well, a long time ago, he gave me lots of advice, and your daddy too."

"You knew my dad?"

"Your daddy didn't have any brothers and sisters and neither did I. I know that you and Virge are buddies, but your dad and I were tighter than ticks. We did a whole lot together and got into all kind of trouble together."

That sure got my attention. "What kind of trouble?

Joe laughed. "You'll just have to ask him yourself."

Virge came out with the lemonade. He bought ice in large chunks and kept it in an ice cupboard. The ice was chipped up and his concoction was in large, blue, aluminum glasses. I remember that my mom and dad gave those glasses to Virge for Christmas. The glasses were cold and dripping wet. It was about the grandest lemonade ever. He handed us the glasses and pulled up a rocking chair.

"I heard you two boys talking. Do y'all think Virge gives too much advice."

Almost together, we replied, "No."

"Good, because I just thought up some more. Do you remember what Joe told you about shooting that sardine can?"

"Yes, he said when what you're shooting at something moving, you don't shoot at where it is, but you shoot at where it's going to be."

"Yep, that was good advice for shooting, but I was thinking that it was pretty good advice for living too. In life, you don't always shoot at where you are, you shoot at where you want to be. Does that make sense?"

"We both paused. Joe Leslie spoke first. You know, it does. Rabbit and I were talking about his daddy. He and I both went to the war together. When I got out, I shot at where I was and came right back here. I've worked in the same old cotton mills that I've always been at."

Looking at me, he continued. "Your daddy, stopped, looked around and shot at where he wanted to be. He's made a career in the military, became an officer, and can actually retire in a few years if he wants. Lordy, wish I coulda' shot where I wanted to be. Where you going to shoot Rabbit?"

"I don't rightly know, but it's a durn good question. I'll have to think on it."

Virge smiled. "Joe, you is a young man, and Rabbit, you is just a young boy. I hope you both think on it."

"How about you, Virge? Have you shot where you want to be?"

"Being on this here porch right now, with the two of you, makes ol' Virge positive he is exactly where he needs to be."

Chapter 7

Carol and Good Times

It was good to be out of Grandpa's doghouse after three weeks. When I took his gun out of the sock drawer and blew a hole through the mirror, My Saturday movie matinees came to a halt. He gave me extra chores around the house to pay for the mirror. Apparently, last night, Wednesday, I wiped the slate clean.

I missed going to the movies, and now there's an extra reason for wanting to go. Before, my grandparents dropped me and my cousin Beaver downtown. I know I've mentioned before that Beaver was a pain in the butt. He was at Boy Scout camp for two weeks, so I would be able to go with a real cousin. Her name is Carol.

When I say real, I don't mean to say that Beaver ain't real. I don't understand cousin stuff too well, but Grandma once told me that Beaver was my second cousin, twice removed. My friend, Virge, claimed that most likely, what was removed was brains and good looks.

Carol has brains and good looks. She lives in Jacksonville, Florida. Her mother has some sort of ailment, so Carol is staying with her aunt, practically right next door to me. Her dad is my mom's older brother. We sat together at church the previous Sunday, and the strangest thing happened. Everyone thought we were twins. She's about two months younger than me, so I'm nine and she's almost nine. More than that though, we just look alike. Both of us have blond hair, green eyes and little freckles that flow across our noses. We share an identical red birthmark in our hairline. We've been told that it looks like a little red angel. I overheard Miss Mabel say that she thought we both have the same precocious manner. I'm not sure what she meant, but guess she thinks we're alike.

Anyhow, on Saturday, I was going to the movies with Carol and not stuffy old Beaver. The routine was the same. Grandpa dropped us off at Charlie Joseph's for lunch. We ordered the usual, a chili-dog and a bag of chips and she had a cola, but I like to save that dime for later.

After lunch, we strolled over to the theater. Carol took one look at the sign outside and said, "I've seen the movie. It really stinks. Can't we go somewhere else?"

This stumped me. I never thought about not going to the movies. After a couple of seconds, I shrugged my shoulders and replied, "Okay. I'm sure we'll find something. LaGrange is a big old town. We still need to meet my grandparents at 3:00 PM over at the farmer's supply store."

Carol swept the hair from her face with her hand and smiled. "I bet we can find something to do."

Scrunching my brow I suddenly brightened. "I know what we can start with. There's something here in town that I bet you ain't seen."

Carol asked, "What is it?"

"Just come on and I'll show you." We walked up two blocks and crossed the street, stopping at Kress's Five and Dime. Stepping through the front door, I looked at her and swept my hand. "There it is."

"What," she asked.

"Right there in front of you, the moving stairs."

"Uh, they call those things escalators. I live in Jacksonville. We've got plenty of them."

Well, maybe they are a big thing in Florida, but here in

LaGrange, Georgia, they were unique. It was the only one I'd ever seen. I think Carol could sense my disappointment, because all of a sudden, she brightened and said, "Let's ride it. I didn't say they weren't fun."

So we did. We did everything you're supposed to do on an escalator and a couple of things not. The people in the store didn't seem to mind us walking up the down stairs. I reckon they've seen that before. They drew the line when I slid down the center strip between the up and down. I didn't know that was frowned on. The lady in cosmetics asked, "Where are your parents?" We gave the 'I dunno' shrug of shoulders and left.

Once outside, Carol said, "I know what we can do now."

"What's that?"

“We can walk over to the Sheriff's department. My uncle is the Sheriff."

The County building is across from the town square. I always thought it was a neat building. There is an old, rusty cannon out front and the outside was covered in marble. The corner where you entered the Sheriff's office was in the shade. Sitting on the marble steps in the summer is about as cool a place as you can find. Standing outside the doorway was a tall woman, dressed in uniform. When we got close, she put her cigarette out and said, "Well if it ain't little Miss Carol. I didn't know you had a brother."

"He ain't my brother. He's my cousin Bill. He's staying with his Grandma Louise this summer."

"Oh, I know you. You're the one they call Rabbit. Ya'll two look just alike. Sweetie, your uncle ain't here, but come on in and let me show you off."

We went in, and there was another woman at the desk and a male deputy walking around. They ooh'd and aah'd over the two of us. It was embarrassing. Finally, they took our fingerprints and took a picture. Where they took the picture was the same place where they lined up people going to jail. In the background, the wall was marked in feet and inches, so you would know how tall the person was. We both came in a little over four feet. I bet they don't get many criminals our size.

I later found out that they developed the picture and it's hanging on the wall at the Sheriff's office. Carol put up her two fingers, 'V' shaped behind my head. It made me look like a devil or something.

After that visit, we walked over to the Army store, one of my favorite places. There is all sorts of military stuff. We tried on army field jackets and helmets, both too big. I had to laugh at Carol. The helmet kept slipping down the front of her face.

Finally, a big, porky guy walked over and asked, "Are y'all going to buy something?" That earned another 'I dunno' shoulder shrug. We left.

"I guess we should head over to the farmer's supply store. We need to meet my grandparents in about thirty minutes."

It's a fun place to hang out. They know me there, so we each got a free cola and were told to make ourselves at home. There are always baby chicks, baby quail, rabbits and other stuff to play with. My grandparents got there soon after we arrived.

When we got in the car, Grandma asked, "Did you have fun?"

We replied in unison, "Yes Ma'am." I was glad she didn't ask if we liked the movie.

Carol was going to stay for supper, so we headed back to Grandma's house. When we got there, the two of us went upstairs to a room my grandmother called the widow's walk. The room jutted out over the front porch. It was a neat room that had tall windows around three sides. The windows in front opened wide, so the room was bright and breezy. We were sitting together on an old coaster bench. The chain links made a noise like a squeeky bucket, *eeenh, eeenh, eeenh, eeenh.* I swear, that noise and motion could almost put you to sleep.

Carol finally said, "I had a great time. It was a fun day."

Smiling, I replied, "We did have us a good old time. I bet we're the only people around here who've been fingerprinted and had our picture taken at the jail."

"I reckon that we probably are."

We rocked some more, *eeenh, eeenh, eeenh, eeenh.*

Finally, Carol asked, "All you've got are brothers, right?"

"Yeah"

"Well, all I've got are sisters, so I've never seen a boy's private parts. Maybe we should take a peek at each other."

` All of a sudden, the breeze died. I felt like everything slowed down. There was a funny, stirring feeling at my mid-section. Stuttering, I said, "Okay."

We both slowly reached for the top buttons of our pants. The magic moment was interrupted by my grandma as she hollered up the stairs, "Are y'all up there?"

In unison, we replied, "Yes, Ma'am."

She continued, "What are y'all doing?"

Once again, in unison, we replied, "Nothin'."

"Well, come on back downstairs and do nothing."

I saw Virge, the next morning. He asked, "Did you and

the Beaver go to the movies yesterday?"

"No, he's at scout camp. I went with my cousin, Carol. We didn't go to the movies, we just walked around and stuff."

"Oh yeah, I remember Carol. Ain't she your Uncle Chuck's oldest girl? If I recall, she is real cute."

"Yeah, she's Uncle Chuck's girl and she is cute. I think when I grow up, I'm going to marry Carol."

Virge chuckled before replying, "You can't marry Carol, cause she's your first cousin."

"Yeah, so what."

"Well, Rabbit, it's against the law to marry your first cousin."

I had to process this bit of news for a while. Finally, I said, "Last month, you told me that it used to be legal to own people, that your own mama was a slave. It don't make any sense to be allowed to own somebody and it sure don't make sense to not be able to marry your cousin."

Virge shook his head and spat a stream of tobacco. "Slavery has been against the law for near a hundred years. Laws is laws. There ain't no law that says they gotta make sense."

I thought it through for a minute and just shrugged my shoulders. "It still don't seem right." What I was thinking though was more important to me at the moment:

I wonder if I'll ever get to see Carol naked?

Chapter 8

The Way with Chickens

When you live on a farm, you shouldn't name the animals. There's a good reason. You might have to eat it. My favorite was a chicken I named Ernest. Virge told me the name didn't make sense since Ernest was really an Ernestine. I don't know, a chicken is a chicken.

Ernest was my favorite because he was so different. The other chickens looked kind of prissy. They'd throw their butts up in the air, hold their heads high and strut. Ernest jerked his head back and forth and rather than strut, shuffled. For some reason, the other chickens hated him.

One day, I came out and found the other chickens pecked Ernest around his wing and back. His feathers roughed off where you could see flecks of blood on his bare skin. My grandpa had a bottle of purple medicine he used to swab on the mules and cows, so I thought it would be perfect for chickens. Ernest always let me pick him up, so grabbing him, I applied the purple salve and sent him on his way.

The next morning, Virge and I were picking figs for my

grandma. The fig bushes were next to the chicken pen. They were thick and ripe. Some fell to the ground and rotted, the smell pungent. We'd gather the good ones and toss the not so good over to the chickens.

At the end of the pen was what looked like a muddy lump. Walking over to take a look, it wasn't a lump. It was Ernest. He was dead. Where I'd brushed the purple salve on was more than bare, bloody skin. You could see the bones.

Virge knows a lot about country stuff, so I asked him, "Why did the other chickens kill Ernest?"

His answer was so much like many of his comments. There was a long pause, a shrug of his shoulders and then the reply. "Sometimes critters kill one another because they're different. With purple salve on his wing, old Ernest was even more different. The others saw it and just came over and pecked him to death."

"Oh, no, he's dead and it's my fault."

"No, child, you wasn't responsible. It was going to happen no matter what. We should have culled Ernest out a long time ago. Animals just don't cotton to others that are different, even of their own kind. It's just the way of life."

"Well, that's just stupid. It don't make any sense at all."

"No, I s'pose not. It's just the way with chickens. Let's finish picking these figs for your grandma."

We continued, either throwing them into a bucket or over the fence to the chickens.

"I think we've picked most of the good ones. Let's just set down a spell and talk about things."

I liked it when Virge explained things. Most grownups just told you, "Do this, don't do that, blah, blah, blah." Virge didn't beat you over the head or anything, he'd just explain things. He'd talk to you and let you decide. I didn't always see things his way, but mostly did. A few weeks ago, when I got my new BB gun and shot a redbird, Virge didn't tell me to not shoot birds, he just explained the life of the bird and because of what I've done, the bird wouldn't never have no family. When he explains stuff, I mostly just shut my mouth and listen.

Before we settled in on the bench, Virge went over to the well and fetched us both a tin cup full of cool water.

"Do you remember your first week here this summer when we talked about my mama being a slave?"

"I do remember, and it still don't seem right that one human being could own someone else."

"No, it sure don't, but it happened right here all around us. As far as I know, all the slaves were black people. I suppose that some of the black folks were treated good, they was fed and had a place to sleep, but they was still slaves. Some were mistreated, beaten and families were split apart. Why do you reckon that white people felt it was right to own black people?"

"I don't reckon I know."

"Okay, let me ask you this, do you think I'm a whole lot different from you?"

"Sure.... You're an old, old, man and I'm just a boy."

Smiling, Virge said, "Well you got that right. I'm older than dirt. What a lot of folks would tell you though is a big difference between us is I'm black and you're white. It could be a reason why white people felt it was alright to own black people. They was different."

Virge spat some tobacco juice right on a cricket. It was amazing how he could aim that stuff.

"About one month after we talked about slaves, you got your BB gun."

My face got red because I thought for sure, Virge was going mention about me killing that bird. He didn't. Instead, he asked if I remembered how Joe Leslie set up all the targets for us to shoot. I did, because we had us a good old time.

"Do you remember when Joe said that he and your daddy went into the military together?"

"Yes, I do."

"You know, it is 1960 now, and I remember 1943 like yesterday. Your daddy and Joe were best friends. They went to volunteer together for the Army. They only asked that they would keep them together. The Army said, "Sure, no problem." The only time them two were together was on the bus to Columbus, Georgia. They sent your daddy to Fort Benning, Georgia and they sent Joe to Montford Point, North Carolina. They didn't see each other again until 1946, right up the hill on my porch."

"How come the Army lied to them?"

"I don't rightly know, but in those days, Army basic training was in different places for white folks and black folks."

"How come?"

Virge smiled before replying, "I reckon cause they was different."

"What I can tell you is those two boys sat on my porch, talked a bit and cried."

"Cried? Why did they cry?"

"It's hard for me to tell you to this day. Let me start with Joe. He knew how to drive trucks, so he wound up serving in the 590th Ambulance Company, first in Britain, then in Belgium and Germany. In 1945, Joe and his unit arrived at a place called Bergen-Belsen. They found mass graves, some not even closed up. The graves was full of skeletons. It was mostly Jews, and those not in the graves were either dead or near dead."

Up on our porch, Joe looked at me, tears in his eyes, and asked, "How can men do that sort of thing to other men?"

"Rabbit, you know how big and tough Joe is? When he asked me that, it brought tears to my own eyes. Then, your daddy started.

"He talked about his air unit fire bombing Tokyo. Government doctors told those young boys that it was okay to bomb the cities, because the Japanese wasn't making weapons in the factories no more, they was doin' it in peoples homes.

"You know what?"

"No, what?"

"It was a lie. They weren't makin' nothin' in their homes. All the young Japanese men were somewhere with the war. Most of what was left was old people and children. Your daddy said the first group of bombers dropped big bombs to break things up. The second group dropped barrels of thickened gas wrapped around by small bombs that caused the fuel to splatter when it hit the ground. They didn't know it, but at the time there was thirty-mile-an-hour ground wind. In other words, they broke the city up then burnt it."

"Why did the government lie to them?"

"I reckon because they didn't know how else to convince nineteen and twenty-year-old kids to kill over one-hundred-thousand old men, women and children. Your daddy recalled he could smell the burning bodies, even at twenty-thousand-feet. After that story, your daddy cried. I went in to get some whiskey to go into all of our water cups. We all sat there, takin' a sip from time to time, rockin' and cryin'."

Shuddering a tear myself, I asked Virge, "How can one man do that to another man?"

"You thought it was stupid when a chicken killed another chicken, just because he was different?"

"Yeah, I did."

"Well, it ain't really different with men. We just talked about slavery and owning people because they was different.

Both of the countries that your daddy and Joe fought against was killing people just because they was different. Think about it for a minute. A chicken is a dumb old thing, but something in its blood just makes it want to kill another chicken that's different. It's troublesome. Why do you suppose a man wants to kill or abuse another man just because he's different?"

"I don't rightly know. Why?"

Spitting a stream of tobacco, Virge said, "I reckon it's in a man's blood too."

Chapter 9

To Kill a Fly

My Grandma Louise and Grandpa Horace were going to spend the weekend in Atlanta. Grandpa had to attend a pre-retirement workshop with the rail company. I suppose I should have been happy for them to get away, but I wasn't. It meant spending the weekend with my other grandparents.

Don't get me wrong, my other grandparents, Nan and Pappy, were great. They only lived three miles from where I stayed. Their property was in the country and had all sorts of fun things. There was a farm, lots of animals, a great barn and a wonderful creek to swim in. One small problem; their place was where my older brother JJ was spending the summer.

I was dropped off at my grandma's. She gave me a big hug and ushered me into the kitchen. Sitting down at the table and sipping on a big, iced glass of Double Cola, we talked a bit. Her first question, probably a good one, "Why don't you and JJ get along?"

I chewed on my fingernail before replying, "Grandma, have you ever seen Flash Gordon at the movies?"

With a puzzled look, she replied, "Yes, why do you ask?"

"Well, I figure that wherever JJ is staying is the planet Mongo and he is Ming the Merciless."

With a smile, she said, "Well, we're just going to keep the two of you apart. You can sleep downstairs in the bedroom next to mine. JJ is sleeping upstairs."

My grandparents were the last people on earth who didn't have a television set. I didn't mind one bit. After dinner, we would all gather in the living room. The walls were lined with handmade, dark stained, bookshelves, overflowing with books. Since this was Saturday night we would listen to a radio show called Midwestern Hayride. My grandpa, (Pappy), had a radio that was about as big as the television set we had at home. He would turn it up loud for the country music and some of the corniest jokes ever. If we behaved, we could stay up and listen to either Gunsmoke or Ranger Bill.

I especially liked Gunsmoke. You didn't need a TV. I liked to stretch out on the small sofa and close my eyes. It was like I could see everything. You could hear the horses clip-clopping, the glasses clinking in Ms. Kitty's bar and the sounds of fist fights or guns fired. Marshal Dillon was talking to Chester that night and said, "I didn't want to shoot him, but dag burn it, he deserved it." In the semi-darkness, I opened my eyes and glared at my brother.

The next morning started out okay, but JJ and I managed to start arguing before breakfast was over. He was telling me that the leaves on a china berry tree were brown. The whole world knows they are green. He was colorblind like crazy, so if that's what he saw, that's the way it was.

My grandma had enough. "JJ, china berry trees are certainly green. You two are just going to have to quit arguing. I can see why your mama wanted you two separated. I've got a job for you after breakfast that I hope will keep you occupied."

JJ has always been shifty-eyed. This morning was no different. With a glint, he asked, "What kind of job?"

"Well, you just finish your breakfast and I'll show you."

After breakfast, Grandma led us to the back patio. It was made of old brick crisscrossed with light green moss. Shaded by a big old magnolia tree, it was cool, and this time a year smelled like sweet lemons. Five weathered, red, Adirondack chairs were grouped around a homemade round table. Grandma handed each of us a fly-swatter.

She explained the job. "I've got some ladies coming over today after lunch and we'll all want to sit outside and enjoy the shade of the patio. I want you two to kill flies. Each one of you keep your own stack of dead flies. Later on, I'll give you a penny for each fly you kill."

Old shifty-eyed, JJ asked, "It don't seem like it would do much good to kill one fly. How come you want us to do it?"

"Well, Mr. Smarty, I'll tell you. More than half of the flies are females, and each female can lay 1,000 eggs during her lifetime. More than half of those eggs become more female flies which in turn will lay 1,000 more eggs. If the fly you kill is a male fly, he can never fertilize any more eggs. Even you should understand that killing that one fly can eliminate millions in the future."

"Hmm, if each one can keep millions from being born, it should be worth more than a penny."

"Don't you worry about the math. JJ, you sit in the left corner, and Rabbit, you sit in the center by the round table. I'll bring you some ice-water in about an hour to see how you're doing."

I didn't care what JJ thought. To me, a penny per fly seemed a good deal. It's easy for me to focus on things, especially when there's money involved. I was getting into it. Looking at my stack of flies, I counted twenty-five. It was impossible to tell how many JJ had, but it didn't look like many.

Despite my concentration, it became obvious that the glass of milk and glass of juice I had for breakfast needed to be relieved. Glaring at JJ, I said, "I've got to go to the bathroom.

Don't mess with my flies while I'm gone."

I came back out a few minutes later. A quick glance at my fly pile revealed a crime. With fury, I turned to JJ and said, "Okay, butt-face, you took some of my flies."

"No I didn't. You must not have killed them good. They just revived themselves and flew off."

With that lame explanation, I swatted the biggest fly on the patio, JJ. The fight began. The loud commotion brought Grandma Nan out to the patio.

"My God, I can't leave you two together for one hour and already you're fighting. What in the world happened?"

"When I went in to go to the bathroom, JJ stole some of my flies."

"Is that right, JJ?"

"No, Ma'am. I reckon that he just didn't kill them good enough and they flew away."

"That doesn't seem likely, but I don't have time to referee. I'm going to give each one of you a quarter. JJ, you go down to the old house and help Pappy clean it up. Rabbit, you go to the garden and pull worms off the tomatoes and beans. Put the worms in a can so you can feed them to the chickens."

We both went our own ways. It was better to be up in the garden by myself than around JJ. Truth be known, I loved working in the garden. When with my other grandparents, there were daily chores for me in the garden. Saving the worms for the chickens was a new one for me though. After pulling just a few worms and giving them to the chickens, it was obvious they loved them. Small surprise that my grandma let the chickens run free range through her garden. There wasn't a single worm low to the ground.

If you looked out across the garden, you could see heat waves rise from the ground. I was about ready to take a water break when the neatest bug possible appeared on a tomato plant. It was a long bug, green in color and had two long, spiked forelegs. It was almost invisible and was faced away from me. It rotated its head all the way back and was looking at me with two huge eyes. I whacked it with a stick.

Picking up my find, I rushed to find my grandmother. She was sitting on the patio, flyswatter in hand.

Yelling, I called out, "Grandma, Grandma, I killed a baby dinosaur."

"You what?"

"I killed a baby dinosaur." Holding my treasure out, I said, "Here it is."

"Oh Rabbit, that's not a baby dinosaur. That's a preying mantis. Your grandpa buys mantis egg casings every year and spreads them through the garden. They hatch and then begin to devour insects. Mantises are good things, not something to be killed. They're a thing of wonder."

About that time, a grim-faced, Pappy was walking up the hill with JJ.

Grandma asked, "What's wrong?"

Shaking his head he said, "Oh nothing much. JJ was just playing with matches and almost burned the old house down. No real harm. I'll just leave the windows open a few days for the smell to go out."

Looking at Pappy, Grandma said, "Our daughter raised JJ, Rabbit and Bubba and now has one more on the way. All of this, and she still retains her sanity." She winked.

“We need to contact the Pope. There's a saint among us."

Chapter 10

Fighting and Family

When you live in the country, you don't need an alarm clock. Roosters crow, cows bellow and my Grandma, Nan, was banging pots around in the kitchen. I knew I should get up, but wanted to lay there for awhile. After all, it was time for plotting. Today after breakfast, I was going to kick my brother, JJ's butt. Lord knows it's time.

I couldn't get the fly killing job out of my mind. The more I thought about, the madder I got. It didn't matter what bull crap story JJ had, we all knew he stole my flies. My brother beat on me a lot, but today was going to be *my* day

It didn't take long for the battle to begin. Right after breakfast, the two of us were standing out on the patio, the scene of yesterday's crime. JJ piped up, "You know, you're such a tattletale. It's like you couldn't wait to blab your mouth about your stupid flies."

"It's not being a tattletale when you tell the truth. You stole my flies."

"Yeah, so what are you going to do about it?"

"What I'm going to do is whip your butt. Let's go up behind the barn and get this over with."

JJ looked surprised.

"It's stupid for us to go up there and fight. You know if we do, I'll win and you'll go blabbing to Grandma."

"Nope, not today. Let's go."

There was a holding pen for calves up behind the barn, surrounded by a wood-slatted fence, about five-feet high. There hadn't been any cows in it for awhile, so was mostly dry. Georgia red clay dust was mixed with dirt and dried cow poop. JJ and I slipped inside and got down to business. Like two wary gladiators, we circled each other in the old pen. Each footfall stirred up puffs of red dust. I felt confident. My armor was much better, with long pants and hard leather brogans. JJ was in shorts and wearing tennis shoes. He feinted, I feinted and as he tried to move in, I kicked him in the shins with my hard leather shoe. He squealed and grabbed his leg. As he did, I hit him in the side of his head. The start was good, but it didn't end well.

Hollering, JJ bull-rushed me. In seconds, I was knocked to the ground. Turning me face down, he shoved my head into the mixture of soil and old cow poop. Pinning me securely with his knees, he started to pummel the side of my head and body. It was weird hearing his hard breathing and the thumping sounds of fists hitting my body.

All of a sudden, I heard a voice. "All right, Mr. JJ, that's enough. Stop it right now."

JJ got a couple of more licks in and then I realized he had been lifted off me. It was Virge.

"Mr. JJ, I told you the fight was over. You just stop now and go on back to the house."

JJ stood back and yelled, "Okay, you little punk. I'm going to get you for kicking me in the leg. Your big, black friend ain't going to be there to help you."

Virge turned toward JJ saying, "Mr. JJ, I done told you to get on home. If you ain't careful, I might just whup your butt myself."

"Yeah, and if you do, I'll tell my daddy."

Virge laughed. "You too smart for dat. Your daddy would giggle in your face and beat your butt again. Now, get along."

JJ left and Virge helped me to my feet, brushing dirt off my face. I turned and asked, "What are you doing here? You live over at my other grandma's."

"Pappy come by to get me early this morning. He wanted me to help him fix the pump at the barn. Maybe you're lucky I showed up."

"I didn't need your help. I was doing just fine."

"Rabbit, your heart was in it, but you just ain't big enough. You might be someday, but today's just not your day. Why do you always fight with Mr. JJ?"

"Because, I ain't going to let him pick on me. I'd rather get a beating than have him get away with all his bull crap."

"Okay, I understand. Let's just go on back to the pump house and clean you up a bit. Your grandma'd be upset seeing you roughed up like this."

We walked to the pump house behind the barn. He sat me down on a hay bale and went to pump some water in a bucket. He also filled two tin cups, one for each of us. It was late summer and the water was cool. He pulled a handkerchief from his pocket. After dipping it into the water, he washed my head and face.

"Rabbit, how come you and Mr. JJ was fighting?"

"I reckon it was stupid. Yesterday, Grandma Nan had us killing flies. We piled them into our own piles, and she was going to pay a penny apiece. When I went to the bathroom, the stupid jerk stole some of my flies. He'd rather steal than work."

"You know Mr. JJ's a lot older and bigger than you?"

"I know, but I thought this time might be different. I'm so tired of him, I feel like killing him. I wish he was dead."

"You don't need to talk like that. Mr. JJ is your brother. You've got to love your brother. Why don't you ask your grandma if you can go to church with me and Carrie and Joe. It's a special day with a Reverend out of Atlanta. Might do you some good."

For the last three summers, I went to church with them most Sundays. I was pretty sure it would be okay. When I got home to my Grandma Louise's on Saturday night, I asked, "Can I go to church with Virge tomorrow?"

"Sure, but how come you don't like coming to our church anymore?"

"I like going to church with you and Grandpa, but it's more fun going with Virge."

Smiling, my grandma smoothed my hair down. "It's just good you want to go to church. I have this vision in my mind of the preacher looking out and seeing you out there. You must stand out like a marshmallow in a plate full of brownies."

I didn't tell Grandma all the stuff I enjoyed. First, just getting there. We drove over with Joe. He drove a 1949, Ford pick-up, painted bright red. I got to sit in the truck bed, usually with Virge. When we got there, I loved seeing the choir come into the church. They wore robes, and came in swayin' and rockin' to the songs, each person with a hand on the shoulder of the person in front of them. Each time, they sang, '*I'm bound for the Kingdom*.'

I don't remember all the words, but at the end of each verse, everybody in the church joined in. I do remember how it ended up.

"Well I'm going to a country where they say we'll never die

Twill be endless joy and glory there for me (*there for me)*

Yes I know I'll live forever in that city in the sky

Well, I'm bound for the Kingdom of the free (*of the free)*."

You would have never thought Virge could sing, but he could. When he and I sang our parts, I tried to lower my voice to match his, but never could do it. Miss Mabel once told Virge he sang like an angel. I'm not sure about that, though he was pretty good.

An always favorite part was when church was over. Food! Virge told me this Sunday was hot dog day.

As usual, the start and middle of the sermon seemed pretty much the same, no matter what church. Some old guy would talk about heaven and hell and what sort of things might get you sent one way or the other. Different folks, same old stories.

Church started, and after the first song, the preacher started laying it on. I had to take a peek at Virge. The old preacher was talking about Cain and Abel. It crossed my mind that maybe Virge put him up to it. I listened for a minute or two, but it was late July. No air conditioning, so in spite of several fans, it got toasty. I was sitting between Virge and Carrie. Leaning into Carrie, I nodded off.

Startled by a loud clapping of hands, I jerked my head up. The preacher was robed. Swerving toward me, his arm and long, bony finger jutted out of the long sleeve of the robe. Pointing right between my eyeballs, he shouted, "Do you want to go to heaven?"

What could I do? I jumped right up and hollered back,

"Yes!"

My answer was greeted by a loud chorus of Amen's and a few Hallelujahs. I could feel my face redden as I sat down.

When church was over, we all headed outside. Before the service, hickory wood was lit in a long, concrete block, barbecue pit. The wood had burned down to big, almost white, hot coals. Hot dogs were splayed across the top of the grill. A wonderful aroma of wood smoke and burning fat filled the air. Virge and I always picked the same kind of dog; swollen, split and slightly blackened on the outside.

I filled my plate with hot dogs, cole-slaw, baked beans and huge homemade dill pickles. I joined Virge who was sitting on the tailgate of Joe's truck. It was a prime spot, under the canopy of a huge live oak. After taking my first bite, I asked, "Did you put the preacher up to talking about Cain and Abel?"

"No, I didn't, but it did sort of fit. Have you been thinking and praying some about what you said about your brother?"

"Yes I have. I know I love JJ, but he sure can be aggravating."

Finished with lunch, Virge reached into his pocket and pulled out a small, rectangular can of Sir Walter Raleigh tobacco. Tamping it into his pipe, he held a match to it. It fascinated me to watch the flame go down and back up.

Taking a puff, Virge said, "I know Mr. JJ can be worrisome to you. At the same time, I can tell you I wish my brother was around to aggravate me. He died when I was seven years old. I miss him every day."

"Rabbit, you and me get to talk from time to time, and it makes this old man happy you mostly listen. When you get to be as old as me, you've learned a bunch of stuff. I want to tell you about family. Family is the most important thing in life.

Your brothers, mama, daddy, and grandma and grandpa, they's all family, but you got lots more. Family also includes everybody in this world who loves you and you love back. One thing I know for sure is if you ain't got family, you ain't got nothin'.

“Does that make sense?"

"Yes it does. I reckon you and me are family too?”

Virge took a couple of puffs on his pipe, I didn't think he was done, so I just sat there and enjoyed the sweet, cherry smell of the tobacco.

Virge answered, "Yeah, I reckon we are.

"You know I'll be going back to school in a month.”

“Yep, I don't know how it happened, but summer is durn near over.”

“When I get back to school, you reckon I oughta' tell my friends I got me an old black brother, or maybe an old black uncle?”

With a twinkle in his eye and a chuckle, Virge said, "Rabbit, if I wasn't so full of hot dogs, I would catch you and whup you."

Chapter 11

Owl Capers

Shoot, I should play for the New York Yankees. I was in Grandma's driveway playing home run derby. Rather than a bat and ball, I was using a stout hickory stick, and throwing up rocks to hit. If I hit it across the road out front, it was a home run. A really good baseball player might have a batting average of .300. I figure mine was about .750! I rarely missed the rock.

Stopping, I looked up the road to the right. Virge was walking from the town side. He never came from that direction, so I put my stick down to go greet him.

"Hi Virge, what you doin'? I ain't used to seeing you walk in this direction."

"Hi, yourself. You know I drive in to town with your grandpa every Thursday. He got me the job of cleaning up the train station once a week. Usually I wait and ride home with him. Today I got done early, so got a ride home with Miss Mabel. She lives on the town side, so I come this way."

"I know your grandpa ain't home yet. He had a heck of a day today."

"Why, what happened."

"It's gonna be a long story. Let's go sit in the shade. I'll get me a drink of water at the pump house and tell you all about it. You're going to like it."

Well, that got my curiosity up. We walked to the pump house. Virge has a tin cup that's just his. My grandma told me if I want a drink a water, I needed to go in the house and use a glass. Most times, I just borrow Virge's cup. I'm pretty sure he don't mind. He poured himself a cup full and we sat on a bench shaded by a big ol' magnolia tree.

"Here goes... Your grandpa picked me up this morning before sun-up. He's got to get to the station early. After we'd driven a little ways, it was like a shadow fell out of one of the trees on the road. All of a sudden, 'WHUMP' and something big hit the front wind shield. Me and your grandpa both ducked."

"What was it?"

"Give me a minute and I'll tell you." Virge slurped some water and got back to his story. "We both got out of the truck to see what it was. There was a big ol' lump of feathers layin' on the side of the road. We went and took a look. It was the biggest dang owl either one of us ever saw. Your grandpa said he thought it was a great horny owl. He asked me to pick him up and put him on the floorboard of the truck. He wanted to show it to all his buddies at the station. I did, and we headed out."

"How big was it? Was it bigger than a chicken?"

"Chicken nothin'. This old boy was bigger than a turkey. That's why he wanted to show it off. Anyhow, we got to the station. He signed in and we both grabbed us a cup of coffee. Your grandpa started walkin' around the station. I can hear him now."

"Hey boys. I want you to walk out to my truck and take a look at what Virge and I come across this mornin'. We hit and killed the biggest dang owl you ever seen. I brought it in. Come on out and take a look."

"They all headed out to the truck. When we got close, it looked like things wasn't quite right. The truck was rockin' and you could see somethin' movin' around inside. The durn bird wasn't dead. He was makin' all sort of a ruckus. We edged closer and you could see he'd ripped up some of the seat and there was bird poop all over the place."

"Your grandpa's friend said, 'Let me go out to my truck and get my pistol. Y'all can crack the door open and I'll shoot him.'"

"Now, weren't no body asking my opinion. I'd have just let that big old beautiful bird go, but they was all hatchin' up a plan."

"The man with the pistol was Mr. Clete. I'm sure you know him. Anyhow, he come back with his pistol and asked your grandpa to slowly open the door. He did, and Mr. Clete proceeded to stick his gun in. I guess Mr. Owl saw an opening and made the most of it. He squeezed through the door just as the gun went off. BOOM. He missed the owl! To me, a good thing. The bullet though, went through the passenger side door, bounced off the pavement, and hit Bubba Thorpe in the leg. Mr. Bubba was grabbin' his leg and hollering, "Ow, Ow, Ow."

"Now Rabbit, you know I ain't one to laugh at no one. Once they figured out Bubba wasn't hurt bad, I truly did want to laugh, but since no one else was laughing, I didn't. The ambulance came, though they just put a big ol' bandage on. The police came and even a newspaper man showed up.

"What happened to the owl?"

Virge laughed now. "I don't rightly know. He was in the truck, got shot at and all sorts of commotion come up. At the end of the thing, no owl, so I reckon he flew away. It was quite a mornin'."

I said, "You've always got somethin' to say about things. How about this one?"

"Well, there might be somethin' here. The thing that comes to mind is, 'You ain't dead til you decides you is.'

Course, I'm kinda partial to, 'Love owls, not pistols.'"

#

For the second time this summer, my grandpa made the newspaper. The headline, 'Local Man Rescues Great Horned Owl.'

I showed it to Virge the next morning and he laughed so hard, he spit his tea clear across the table.

Chapter 12

The Red

When I went to bed last night, I had two brothers. This morning, my grandma hollered up the stairs and woke me up with, "Congratulations! You now have a sister to go with those two nasty brothers."

How about that? I wonder if it will be any different having a girl in the house.

I didn't have to wait long to find out. My day was normal. I did my morning chores and then went with my friend Virge to hunt for arrowheads. It's a good day when you find one arrowhead. We found two. Lunch was special. Many times, we just have sandwiches. Not today. Grandma put out cold fried chicken and left-over potato salad. There were fresh sliced tomatoes on the side, and of course, biscuits.

Maybe I should have known something was up. Grandma patted me on the hand and said, "Grandpa and I are driving over to Alabama tomorrow. Your dad will need some help, and then when your mom comes home with your sister, she will need some help. It's too early for you to visit them, so we're going to leave you here. I'm pretty sure she could see the disappointment in my face. "Now, Rabbit, I know you're anxious to see your new sister, but it isn't a good time."

She read the disappointment right, but it wasn't about my sister. I figured for sure, I would have to go over and stay with my other grandma, which meant time with my brother JJ

I breathed a sigh of relief when she said, "This time, we're going to let you stay here. Miss Erin, from our church, will be staying with you. When you stayed with us two years ago, she played piano in vacation Bible School. In a few weeks, she is going to Macon to teach school. Do you remember her?"

"I think so. Does she have red hair, freckles across her nose and wears braces and glasses?"

"Well, I think you've got the right girl, but she doesn't wear braces anymore and I don't think glasses. Do you think you'll be all right with her?"

"Sure. I'll still be able to visit with Virge won't I?"

"Of course you will, honey. Erin will be coming by tonight, so let's go straighten up the guest bedroom."

Erin arrived after dinner and we got re-introduced. I was a little tongue tied, because she was so pretty. Those freckles were still there, but seemed to flow over her nose like a little speckled rainbow. Her hair flowed long and free, not put up in a pony-tail like it use to be. It was beautiful, red and curly. No braces and no glasses either.

I stammered, "It's nice to meet you again, Miss Erin."

"It's nice to meet you too, Mr. Rabbit. Don't you think we ought to just call each other Erin and Rabbit?"

It made sense. Mr. Rabbit sounded stupid.

She went on, "This is going to be a grand adventure for us both. I grew up with two sisters, so never had a brother. You've never had a sister, so now we can learn together."

When she smiled at me, I had a strange feeling in my mid-section. The feeling reminded me of the time my cousin Carol was about to drop her drawers. I felt pretty sure everything was going to be okay.

The next morning, my grandparents loaded up their Plymouth station wagon and headed to Alabama. Erin and I stood together on the front porch and waved goodbye. She looked down at me and said, "Your grandma told me you have chores every morning. Would you like for me to help you?"

"You could, but they're not hard. It's just taking care of the chickens and seeing if any beans or tomatoes need picking. Plus, I don't see you helping me dressed like you are."

She paused for a moment and then laughed. "I guess you think I'm a silly city girl. I don't suppose a sundress and sandals are the best thing for farm wear. I do have some jeans, tee shirts and sneakers. I'll change."

As I was brushing my teeth, I heard Erin cry out, "Ouch, ouch!"

Running in to her room, I shouted, "What's wrong?"

"I was just raising my window and I got stung by two huge hornets. I didn't know it would hurt so bad."

The guest room wasn't used too often. I walked over and could see some agitated wasps flying around a small nest at the corner of the window.

"Erin, let's go out to the kitchen. Those ain't hornets, just wasps. They'll calm down after awhile and I can spray em. For now, I can help ease the pain of those big stings on your arm."

On the way to the kitchen, I grabbed a package of my grandpa's chewing tobacco. I sat her down in a chair and cut a small plug of tobacco off. Putting the tobacco in a coffee cup, I poured a small amount of water on it, added some baking soda and mashed it down with a spoon. When it formed a paste, I applied it over the part of her right arm that was red and swole up.

She was looking at me with a puzzled look the whole time. Finally, she said, "You know, the pain has gone away. Who taught you this?"

"My friend Virge Gates taught me this summer when I got stung by a bunch of yellow jackets."

"Is Virge a boy who lives nearby?"

"He lives nearby, but he ain't no boy. Virge is ninety years old. You can see the corner of his cabin from the front porch. It ain't even a half mile away. He helps my grandma and grandpa out around the farm. You can meet him today. He was going to come by and take me fishing. Would you like to go?"

"I'd love to go. I've never been fishing and Virge sounds like an interesting man. Sounds fun."

Virge came by at two in the afternoon. I made the introductions and wasn't surprised Virge knew her. He knew her daddy, mama, grandpa and grandma. "Yes, yes, Miss Erin. I remember you as a little girl." Within minutes, it was like they were the best of friends.

Halfway down to the lake, Virge suddenly stopped. "Oh my goodness, here's a treat for both of you. Close your eyes and open your mouth for a big surprise."

Dumb I guess, but we both closed our eyes and opened our mouths, Virge put something about the size of a small apple into our mouths and said, "Take a bite." It wasn't no apple, it was a green persimmon.

For a minute, think about putting the bitterest lemon you've ever had in your life in your mouth and taking a big bite. Think about how your face would scrunch up and you almost suck your lips back into your mouth. Get the picture in your mind and know the green persimmon was ten times worse. I heard Erin screech, "ugh" and then she spit it out. I did the same.

All the while, Virge was laughing. I could see Erin was smiling, but I was mad. I never yell at Virge, but I did this time.

"What do you think is so funny. Whatever we put in our mouth tastes terrible."

"Rabbit, I couldn't help myself. My daddy did the same thing to me about eighty years ago. I never thought about it till we walked by the Persimmon tree. If you could have seen your faces, you might have thought it funny too. Plus, you know how old Virge likes to give lessons and I reckon there's a lesson in this one too."

"Yeah, I learned the lesson alright. Don't trust nobody."

"No, the message is much simpler. Don't never close your eyes and open your mouth."

Virge started laughing again, and this time, Erin was joining in. Not me.

"I still think it was mean."

"Well, it would hurt me for you to stay mad. Would it be better if I took a big old bite of a green persimmon for you?"

I thought about this for a moment before I replied, "Yeah, I reckon so."

True to his word, Virge pulled a big green persimmon off, closed his eyes, opened his mouth and took a big bite. The effect was almost immediate. His cheeks pooched in and his mouth formed a tight little 'O'. I have to admit, I laughed. He looked weird.

"So now you think it's funny?"

"I sure do. You should have seen the way you looked. Your face normally looks like a prune. Now it looks like a dried up old prune with wrinkles on top of the wrinkles."

The three of us just howled. After Virge caught his breath, he said, "You know there's another lesson in all this?"

Erin and I looked at each other puzzled. Finally, she asked, "What's the lesson?"

Virge smiled and said, "When friends laugh together, there ain't no room for anger."

He was right, so we headed down to the lake to go fishing.

My grandparents' lake was beautiful, though on the small size by design. When built twenty years ago, the contractor wanted to make it larger. Given its location at the bottom of a natural basin and being spring fed, the contractor said, "We can make fifty acres if you want. It's a natural site." They made it five acres, large enough for lots of fish, but small enough to comfortably canoe around.

Many of the lakes in those days were fed by natural wash. This one, fed by two different springs, was a shade of green and rarely stained like red Georgia dirt. One of the springs even had a name, Little Blue. People in the county would come by and fill jugs with the cool and pure water. A spring in the next county was named, Blue Springs. Owned by a millionaire and developed, it made Little Blue seem a good name.

Virge gave Erin some of the history. Our fishing trip ended when he told her, "Rabbit and I cleaned out around old Little Blue last week. It was so hot, we just went over and soaked our feet in the spring. It don't matter what time of year it is, that old spring just keeps pumping out water at sixty-two-degrees."

Being cool in the middle of a hot Mid-West Georgia summer, made it special. In winter, you could see steam rising, because the temperature tended to be warmer than the outside air. Erin almost squealed when she asked, "Can we just soak our feet first?"

What could Virge say? I've already told you she was real cute.

Anyhow, we headed over to the spring. Over time, it had been lined with rock. There were two large ones that you could sit on. We all went over and took off our shoes.

Trying to be a gentleman, I reminded Erin, "If you want to take a drink, you might want to before Virge and I stick our feet in." A metal dipper hung on an aged cedar post for just that reason. We all took a big drink before sitting down.

As we settled in, Virge asked Erin, "Did I ever tell you about the first time that me and Rabbit went fishing?"

"No, but I wish you would."

"Well, Missy, you just sit back and I'll tell you the story. It's a good one."

"When Rabbit was six years old, he asked me to take him fishing."

"Wait, first you have to tell me how he got the nickname. His grandma told me it came from you."

"I gets to take all the credit. The first time I saw him sittin' on the front porch, it came to me. Those big old eyes was lookin' all around and them big old ears was movin' side to side. He wasn't saying squat. I told his grandma that he was like the rabbit. He was just takin' it all in. Ain't nobody going to get one by the Rabbit. Anyhow, it just stuck."

"Before you go on with the story, the two of you have to come up with a nickname for me."

"Well, Miss Erin, it ain't going to be as clever as Rabbit, but I reckon we ought to call you Red."

I had to pop in. "Wait, wait, wait. Don't you reckon we should come up with a nickname for Virge? I'm for calling him Prune Face."

They both laughed.

"Y'all know that Virgil is my real name, so Virge is the nickname I've gone by all my life, so here goes the story. I told Rabbit that the best bait for fishin' in the lake was worms, and the best place to get them was his grandma's garden where she kept her compost pile. We got us a couple of cans and headed over. I handed Rabbit a shovel. I told him to brush the stuff off'n the top of the pile.

He's a pretty good boy and generally does what you ask. All of a sudden he piped up and said, 'Virge, that ain't stuff. That's cow poop. That stuff is nasty.'"

I told him, "Now Rabbit, ain't nothin' God made nasty. Let me show you something. I brushed the top off the pile and worms started going everywhere. We scooped them up and put them in the cans."

I explained, "God is pretty smart. Them cows poop and your grandma throws it here with all her vegetable trimmings, leaves from the yard and other stuff. Them worms then eat it all up and den dey poop. It becomes that dark ol dirt you see right there. Your grandma take all that dirt and spread it around all her vegetables. It makes em grown big and strong."

He looked at me and said, "That still sounds nasty."

I had to ask him, "Did your grandma make you one of her mater sandwiches for lunch, one of those good un's on white loaf bread, slobbered up with mayonnaise?"

"How did you know?"

"I told him I wasn't no mind reader. The proof was the tomato goop on the front of his shirt! I then told him the science of the whole thing. Rabbit, through dat mater and down through dat dirt, through dem worms, and through all that other stuff, you done et some cow poop!"

After a bout of laughter, Erin asked me, "Do you remember that?"

"I do remember. It seemed a bit dumb to me, but Virge knows a lot about nature stuff. Listening to him, it made sense."

"What else did I teach you that day? I know you ain't forgot, because I see you practice what I taught you all the time."

"Virge told me that I wasn't fishin', I was feedin'. I used to take the whole worm and sometimes two, and wad them all up on the hook. I couldn't figure out why Virge always caught more fish than me. He showed me how to break a single worm in half and string a small part over the barb of the hook rather than a big old blob. That way, when the fish smelled the worm, he'd take a bite and most likely get a part of the hook."

"And what else did I tell you?"

Rolling my eyes, I said, "I really do listen to you sometimes. You told me that fishing was a good lesson in life. Don't matter if it's bait or fish, don't use mor'n you need."

Virge smiled at Red and she gave him a big one right back. She finally said, "When I get to that school in Macon, I hope I can be half the teacher you are, Virge."

We all talked some more and at the end of it, didn't do any fishing. I didn't mind just sitting around. When Virge starts telling stories, I like to just listen. We headed back up the hill, and Virge headed off to his cabin and Red and I went back to the house.

When we got there, she said to me, "That was great. I hope you didn't mind not going fishing. It was just so interesting to hear Virge tell his stories. He's very fond of you. You two made me all sweaty with all that walking around. I'm going to take a bath. Give me twenty minutes and I'll make us some supper."

We split ways, me going upstairs to my bedroom and Red to the downstairs bath. I hung out up there for a while and then headed back down the stairs. When I got near the bottom, I noticed that the door to the bathroom was partially open. Looking through the half open door, I froze in my tracks. My line of sight was to a mirror, but in that mirror, I saw Red. She was buck naked!

Her leg was up on the edge of the bath and she was drying. For the second time since she'd come, I got that strange feeling in my mid-section. I didn't want to keep going downstairs and I didn't want to go back up either. I couldn't move. All of a sudden, she looked up in the mirror and saw me. Taking a step toward the door, she closed it.

My older brother, JJ, tells me lots of stuff. Most of it is trash, but he did tell me there was a certain way you could tell a girl's true hair color. He is often wrong, but maybe not this time. Red was a true red head.

I hustled into the kitchen and started setting the table. In a few minutes, she walked in. She was dressed. She paused for a moment before asking, "You weren't peeking in on me were you?"

I know I blushed when I replied, "No, but I should have told you that this is an old house. It's done settled and relaxed over the years. That bathroom door is going to spring open every time unless you latch it."

Red smoothed her still, wet hair away from her face with her hand. "I believe you, Rabbit, so I should just apologize for embarrassing you."

"You didn't embarrass me."

"I didn't?"

"Well, no. You were the naked one."

"Get over here you rascal and finish setting the table."

We spent three more days together. It was really fun having me an older sister. I believe it was fun for both of us. If you ain't never lived on a farm, you just ain't lived. We did it all. Virge even let her ride one of the mules. I was glad to see my grandma and grandpa get back, but sad too. I knew Red would be going to Macon.

The day they got back, we both helped get things re-organized. We then packed up her car. Standing beside it, she said, "I told you when I got here, I was going to enjoy having a brother. I got more than that. I found a person who was willing to include me in his life and be my friend. We can't really be brother and sister, but can we always be friends. Who knows, maybe I'll be transferred to where you live in Alabama. I could be your teacher."

I had to pause for a minute, smile, and just let life catch up with me. "Red, I would be honored to be your friend for the rest of my life. You just need to know one thing."

With a puzzled look, she asked, "What?"

"You could never be my teacher."

"Why's that?"

“Because, standing in front of that room, it wouldn't matter what you said or how smart you were. I'd always remember how you looked naked."

I believe that Red was taken aback. At least, she stepped back and kind of squinted at me. The squiggle lines on the top of her nose bunched up in ridges. It was a stare down. The first one to blink or smile would lose. It was the nose thing, it really wasn't fair. I lost. Actually, it wasn't a blink, more a wink, combined with the toothiest grin I could conjure up.

She broke up in laughter and tousled my hair. "You know, Rabbit, sometimes I wish you were fifteen years older."

"Me too Red. Me too."

Chapter 13

Snakes

The rooster started his loud greeting, so I knew it was time to get up. I wasn't in no hurry though. My grandparents' house has only one bathroom. I'd been there all summer, so knew the routine by now. Grandma gets there first. Even though they have indoor plumbing, they still have a thunder bucket in their bedroom. The first sound I hear is the sound of that bucket swinging. It sounds like a rusty hinge, *squeak, squeak, squeak*, and then I hear her dumping it. She then does her routine, which is pretty quick. Grandpa's turn is next and God is he loud. There's all sorts of grunting and groaning. It seems strange, but he always clears his throat, hawks into the toilet then pees. He shaves with an old fashioned straight razor. He strops it before each use, *schwap, schwap, schwap.* Once finished, he splashes on Old Spice and I hear, "Ahhhh." When I smell the aftershave, I know it's my turn.

It was a sad day, to start a sad week. There were only seven more days before I'd be heading home to Alabama. To me, the summer seemed to disappear. As bad as the day was for me, little did I know it would be worse for my grandma. Of course, I'd be able to see my new baby sister for the first time. My grandma showed me a picture and asked, "Now, isn't she the cutest thing?"

I've been told I'm a sensitive person. Maybe I am, because I replied, "Yes Ma'am, she sure is." All the time, I was thinking she looked like a shriveled-up frog. Her skinny little hands and fingers were stretched out toward you and her face was all wrinkled and pinched up.

The bathroom was finally free. Finishing up by splashing on Old Spice too, I headed to the kitchen for breakfast. As I was about to round the corner into the kitchen, I stopped. Grandma and Grandpa were arguing, which was very unusual. Grandpa thinks he's the boss, but as far as I could remember, he ain't never been right.

Not that I was eavesdropping, but it didn't seem right to keep going. I heard my grandpa say, "Hell no, I ain't jealous. It's just that I found that note about your boyfriend."

Loudly, my grandma asked, "What in the world are you talking about?"

"Now Louise, I'm not stupid, I found the note. It said, 'Don't forget to pick up Curly Kale.' So, I want to know. Who the hell is Curly Kale?"

I couldn't help myself. I started snickering. From around the corner, I heard my grandma say, "All right, Rabbit, I know you're out there. Come on in."

Glaring at Grandpa, she said, "Even Rabbit knows about Curly Kale."

"He does? How come I don't? Who is he?"

Giggling, I said, "He ain't no he. It's more like an it. Curly kale is that green stuff that Grandma makes that's like turnip greens, only better. We had it two nights ago with fried pork chops. The two of us ate it all up and then sopped up the juice with our cornbread."

With a sheepish grin, Grandpa said, "I knew that. I was just clowning around." He took another bite of eggs and biscuit. Grandma just rolled her eyes. She did pat me on the head.

When Grandpa left to get ready for work, Grandma sat

down and scooted her chair next to mine. She brought her coffee and fixed one for me. Well, I call it coffee, Grandpa calls it cream and sugar with a little coffee for flavor.

"Well, Rabbit, it's your last week here on the farm. We're sure going to miss you."

Her eyes were red and a little misty. I guess she was a bit sad. I felt pretty sad too, but I wasn't going to cry. My eyes were red, just cause I get real bad allergies in late summer, that's all.

"You know, since it's your last week, you don't have to do your chores. I want you to know I've been proud of you all summer. You do your chores each day without complaining or putting them off. You've been a joy."

I sniffled. Those darn allergies.

"I want to do my chores. It's what I do, plus I've gotten used to those dumb old chickens. You reckon they're going to miss me?"

She gave me a big old smile. "I reckon they will."

I went out to my job, first feeding the chickens and gathering eggs. I checked in on the brooder room. There were some new chicks I wanted to see. What I saw was strange. The chicks were gone, or at least mostly gone. There were a bunch of feathers and a half of one chick. From their nest, a head backed out, a big old snake head. Rushing out and looking behind the shed, there was a huge snake coiled up. He just looked at me and flitted his tongue in and out.

Running inside to get my grandmother was troublesome. Even though she lived in the country all her life, she was deathly afraid of snakes. They were her chickens though, so I thought she should know. I explained the situation and she came out. We slowly walked to the brooding pen. She had one foot back so she could turn around and run if need be. We crept around to the back of the pen and looked down at a huge black snake with white rings. You'd think he'd be scared of us, but he was just coiled up, sunning himself and looking proud.

Keeping her foot back seemed to work for her. She shrieked, "Good God!" Quickly turning around, she almost ran me over. When we got around to the front of the shed, she said, "Go get Virge to come kill this snake."

I said, "Grandma, I can kill it if you want. I reckon a shovel ought to do the trick."

She quickly said, "No, I want you to go get Virge. He'll know what to do."

I shrugged my shoulders and went to get Virge. His cabin was about a quarter mile away. I ran, which was pretty much what I did all the time anyhow. Virge was on his front porch in his rocking chair. He saw me and said, "Hey, Rabbit, what you in such a big hurry for this mornin'?"

Catching my breath, I blurted, "A big old snake has got into the brood pen and killed some chicks. Grandma wants you to come kill it."

"Rabbit, slow down a bit. Go on over to the hand pump and get yourself a drink of water."

I filled the dipper and slurped down the cool water.

"Okay, come back and sit on the porch and tell me about this snake."

Sliding onto the step and taking a breath, I began, "It's a big old snake. I bet he's longer than I am tall."

"Okay, let's talk about what the snake looks like. Was his head big and shaped like the head of a shovel?"

"I don't know if it was shaped like a shovel head or a mules butt. It was a snake head and it was connected to a snake. Who gives a shit what his head looked like?"

Virge tapped the ashes out of his pipe before sharply saying, "Now, Rabbit, you know the "S" word ain't somethin' you say. I'm just tryin' to get a feel for what type of snake you got down there. Let me ask you somethin' else. Was he colored up like the ground and leaves, or what?"

Scratching my head, I answered, "He wasn't colored like leaves at all. He was black and had white stripes."

"That's great. What we got is an Eastern king snake. As far as snakes go, they don't come no better."

"Well, are you going to go down and kill it?"

"Naw, I ain't going to kill it. God's got a plan for all of his critters. They've all got a place in this world. I've known your grandma all her life and I know she's scared to death of snakes. Her brother played a mean trick on her when she was about six years old. He put a dead snake all coiled up in the outhouse where he knew she would see it. I could hear her scream all way up at my house. I ran down and got it out."

"Did her brother get in trouble?"

Virge laughed. "He sure did. I whupped him with a switch. He ran off and told his daddy. His daddy came out and asked me for my switch and he whupped him too. Maybe the two of us beat some sense in him. He wound up being a pretty good boy."

"What we're going to do is go get that snake. Old Virge would like to have him as a pet. King snakes are smart. Down there, he's eating chicks which ain't good. I'll put him underneath my house. He'll eat rats and mice. They even eat copperheads and other poisonous snakes."

"What you going to do when he eats up all the mice and rats? I don't believe you got a whole bunch of snakes up here."

"That's a good question and I got a good answer. I'll go catch him some rats or mice. The barn is full of 'em. Shoot, I might even let him sleep over at the barn some time."

"Virge, you say that God's got a plan for all critters, but rats and mice are pretty much worthless ain't they?"

"No, they ain't. You just got to understand the circular

nature of life."

"I don't get it. How can a rat or mouse be important?"

Virge smiled before replying, "Well, a snakes gotta eat."

Chapter 14

Snake Catcher

Hanging around Virge was always fun. You never knew when you were going to learn something new. Today, we were going to catch us a snake.

"Okay, I reckon a snake does have to eat. How are we going to catch it?"

"We? You make it sound like you're going to help old Virge."

"Sure, I'm going to help. I might have to catch me a snake someday. We best be going though. Grandma was kinda antsy."

We headed back down to the big house. About half way there, Virge stopped by a scrubby permisson tree. Reaching into his pocket, he pulled out his Barlow pocket knife and whacked a branch off. He trimmed top and bottom and then held it out.

"I believe this will be just about right." He had about a three-foot-long limb that was straight but had two trimmed branches on the front in the form of a V. The point of the V was about one-half inch wide, and the top was three inches wide.

As we walked, Virge started teaching. "Rabbit, what we got here is a snake picker-upper stick. The snake ain't poisonous, but he can bite. His teeth are small and can't really hurt you, but you never know what he's had in his mouth. This here stick will keep his head away from my hand. I'll trap his head under the V end and then just reach over and pick him up....unless you want to?"

"No, I reckon not this time. Probably best to learn how first."

Virge said, "Yeah, it probably is best for me to do it this time."

As we neared the house, we saw my grandma. Dressed as usual in her cotton dress, she was standing by the hen-house and pointing to the ground. She shrilled, "The damn snake is still there. I'm going in. Do you want me to take the boy with me?"

"No ma'am. He'll be fine here with me."

"You *are* going to kill the snake, aren't you, Virge?"

"Well, Miss Louise, I'm sure nuff going to get rid of him for you."

She said, "Okay," turned, and rushed back to the house. I was glad I wasn't between her and the house. I'm pretty sure she'd have run me down.

As soon as she was out of sight, Virge snuck up on the snake. Sometimes I can't believe how much he knows. Things went exactly like he said they would. Extending the stick, he trapped the snake's head and then reached down and picked him up. The snake immediately curled around the stick. Once wrapped around, Virge trapped his tail end down with his other hand.

I whooped, "Virge, that's slicker than snot. You caught the snake just like you said you would. How come he wrapped back up on your stick?"

Smiling, Virge said, "A king snake is what's called a constrictor. He'll wrap himself around whatever he's after and squeeze til it's dead. Just think, he's probably laughin' and saying, *lookee here, I done caught myself a big old Negro.*

With a big grin, he asked, "Do you want to touch him?

"Heck yeah. I helped catch him didn't I?" Walking over, I touched the snake. I figured that he would be slimy and cold, but he wasn't. His skin was dry to the touch and you could feel his muscles moving beneath his skin. The shiny black color, with the white color bands were pretty.

"Virge, he's a beauty."

"Yeah, he is. Since I'm goin' to take him home with me, we ought to give him a name. Can you think up a good one?"

"Well, you got yourself a snake on a stick. It would sound kind of dumb to name him snake, so why don't we call him Slick?"

"I like that name. Just know that he's your snake too. You go tell your grandma that I got rid of the snake. I don't see no good reason to tell her I took it home and throwed it under my house. You make sure you come by and see me before you go home to Alabama."

"You know I will. I'll have to check in on Slick." It seemed pure, plum, strange watching old Virge walking back to his house. It's not every day you see someone walking around with a snake named Slick, choking a stick.

Grandma was having a bad week. First the snake and now her new dog King. My dog, Skippy, died earlier in the summer. I suppose he wasn't really my dog, since he did live on the farm all the time, but he did seem partial to me. Like people, dogs got personality. Skippy sure did. One day I sat on the front porch in a rocker. I didn't mean too, but rocked over his tail. It didn't make sense to apologize or nothing, it did make sense to run. He chased me until he got close enough to nip me in the butt. Once done and bit, it was all over. I guess he figured we were equal now.

He did have a bad habit of scrunching down in the ditch by the road. When a car would come by, he would jump up and try to catch it. Well, one day, he caught one and it killed him.

Grandma found a replacement, who she named King. He was a mix between a Boxer and a Golden Retriever. Grandpa and I both agreed that rather than King, he should be named Peasant. My grandpa called him Piss-ant, which I reckon is French for Peasant.

King had a problem with cars too. He didn't chase them out on the main road, but when my grandma would back her 1949 Plymouth Deluxe Coupe out of the driveway, King would bite at the tires all the way out the driveway. She was afraid she would run him over. He wouldn't chase Grandpa's truck, just the Plymouth.

Like Virge, my grandpa knows a lot of stuff. He told me one day that King wasn't chasing the car at all. I had to ask, "He ain't? It sure looks like it."

"Nope, you just got to understand dogs. He isn't chasing the car, he's chasing his reflection that he sees in the hubcaps. I know how to get him to stop."

"What are you going to do, Grandpa?"

"Easy-peasy. I'm going to tamp a towel behind the hubcap. When he bites at his reflection, he'll reach out and bite the towel. When he grabs it, he will be shook to hell and back. It'll teach him a lesson and he'll never chase another hubcap."

Grandpa got in the Plymouth and slowly started backing out. King burst out from under the back porch and started chasing the car. All of a sudden, his teeth bit down on the towel. With a growl, he hung on. His body did a half twist and he slid away from the towel. It didn't look like he was moving.

Grandpa got out of the car and yelled, "Durn, I think I killed the piss-ant. We're going to have to tell your grandma that her dog is dead."

"What do you mean *we*, Grandpa? It wasn't my idea, and I wasn't drivin'. I was just watchin'."

"I reckon you're right. I hate it, because I didn't really mean to do it. I know I made fun of the dog, but King was really a pretty good dog."

The minute he said, King, I looked over at the dog that was sprawlled out by the driveway. His tail wagged a little and he lifted his head up. He got up kinda shaky and wandered back to under the porch.

Grandpa leaned back against the car and muttered, "Whew, that was a close one. Does Virge still explain things to you and share advice?"

"Yessir, he sure does."

"Well, I'm going to give you some too. I made a decision without thinking about the bad things that might happen. King could easily be dead rather than shook up. Know that just because a grown-up makes a decision, it ain't the gospel. It could be a bad decision."

What he said made sense, but for sure, King never chased the car out of the driveway again.

Chapter 15

Old Hardy Cemetery

Grandma's and Grandpa's farm was a big one, about two-hundred-fifty acres. During the summer, Virge and I pretty much walked all of it. We'd walk to the lake, look for arrowheads or sometimes even find a lost cow. In the far Southwest corner was about ten acres that we never went to. It was a place called the Old Hardy Cemetery. Summer was near over, so I asked Virge why couldn't we go there. His answer was spooky.

"There be haints there. The last time I was there, I talked to your grandma's great uncle."

"That don't seem likely. Her daddy ain't even alive. How could you be talking to someone even older?"

"Haints is just another word for ghosts. Some folks don't think they is real, but when you done talked to one, you get to believe in em real fast. I wouldn't go back over there for nothin'. Some folks think I'm crazy, but I don't care. I know what I saw."

"If I asked you real nice would you take me?"

"You know you is my friend and there ain't much I wouldn't do for you. Ask your grandma to take you. She goes pretty often. I see her going sometimes with flowers in her hands."

"My grandma is too old to be walking that far."

"Shoot, boy, when cows or calves get lost and you ain't here, who do you think goes lookin' for em. Your grandma, that's who. Over the years, she and I done walked every bit of this property. Well, almost all. I won't go with her to that cemetery, and she knows it."

"What did her great uncle say to you that got you scared? Was it mean or something?"

"No, weren't nothin' mean about it. He just wanted to know if I was watchin' out for Miss Louise. Don't matter if it were mean or not. A person that is dead and buried talked to me just as plain as you are now."

I knew it wouldn't do me any good to convince Virge to take me. When he digs his heels in on something, it's durn near impossible to get him to change his mind. I decided that when I went back to the house for lunch, I would ask her.

"Grandma, over the summer I've pretty much walked on every bit of this farm but one place, the old Hardy Cemetery. Do you reckon we could walk over there?"

She chuckled. "I bet you asked Virge to take you?"

"Yes Ma'am, I did."

"Virge is convinced that the last time he was there, he talked to my great uncle, Robert White. Your brother, Bubba, is named after him. If he ever outgrows his nickname, maybe he'll go by Robert."

"Do you think that he actually talked to him?"

"I don't know child. I do know that he believes that he did. To me, it is a spiritual place. Most of my kin are buried there. There's a nice stone bench. Sometimes I go and sit down with all my kinfolk. I've been about three times this summer. I would have taken you with me, but you're generally somewhere with Virge. Why don't we go tomorrow morning while it's still cool?"

"How can they be your kin? Ain't Grandpa the one named Hardy?"

She laughed. "I'm surprised you never asked. You see,

his name is Hardy too, but he isn't from around here. His family is actually from Mississippi."

Panicked, I asked, "He ain't your first cousin is he?"

"No, honey, the Hardy relatives around here are just yours and mine. How come you're asking?"

"Oh, nothin'."

It was hard for me to get to sleep that night. I kept thinking about ghosts and having the chance to talk to one. If I did, I bet I'll be the only boy in my whole school who talked to a real ghost.

After grandma and I finished our chores. We packed up a little basket and headed to the cemetery. It was a little after nine in the morning, but it was August, so already hot. The walk was about thirty minutes. We got there and grandma suggested that we sit on the bench to catch our breath. In her basket were two small mason jars full of ice water. It tasted great after our walk.

I had been to cemeteries before, but this one was totally different. There wasn't cut grass all mowed and pretty with clean marble headstones. It was in the middle of the woods. There were tall oak and hickory trees, long-leaf pines and magnolias. The magnolias were in bloom, so there was a sweet smell of lemons in the air. A cedar tree in one corner was the biggest one I ever saw. If we have time, I might climb it.

It must have been twenty degrees cooler in the shade. It was still and other than a jay-bird hollering, there wasn't a sound. The ground was covered in a vine I was familiar with, Jasmine. It looked like a green blanket.

"Grandma, this don't look like any cemetery I've been to before."

"Probably not. This one isn't taken care of by anyone other than me, and I can't do as much upkeep as I used to." She pointed to our right. "The newest grave here is over there.

See the one with the cross on top of the stone?"

"Yes Ma'am."

"Walk over and read me what it says."

I walked over and brushed some pine straw off. "It says, Harold Hardy. The dates are 1893 and 1938. It then says, Beloved Son and Brother. He's got our name."

"You see, this is one of the interesting things about an old cemetery. All the graves got a story. A whole lot more than what's written on them. Harold was my brother. If he was still alive, he would be your Great Uncle. I know for sure he would spoil you to death. He was the sheriff for the whole county. One cold night, he was on a manhunt looking for an escaped convict. He caught pneumonia and died--way too young.

Take a look at the grave next to his. What does it say?"

"It says, Dr. John Jackson Hardy, born 1869, died 1936. He's got the same name as Daddy and JJ, so I reckon he's kin too."

"Yep, He was my father. I often wonder if he had been alive when Harold was sick, he might have cured him up. He was the primary doctor for everyone around here. Folks didn't have much money, but he never turned anyone down. Lots of times he would be paid in chickens, eggs, or a smoke-house ham."

"Now, the grave that is two to the right is the one that scared old Virge. Tell me what it says."

"It says Robert White, Captain, Confederate States of America. The dates are 1830 to 1917. Was he in the army or something."

"Yes, he was in the Civil War. That's the one your grandpa calls the war of northern aggression. He's another one that would have spoiled you. He sure spoiled my brother and I."

"There's another grave over here that has a little lamb on

it."

"Yes, I know. What does it say?"

"It says, In Memory and Love for Our Daughter, Ory Elizabeth Smith. Born November 11, 1882, died April 13, 1885. She wasn't even three years old. Do you know what happened?"

"Well, I told you that every grave had a story, and this one does for sure. The way I heard the story is that little Ory's mom and dad tried and tried to have a baby. When she was thirty-nine, little Ory was born. Most women in those days had children in their teens or early twenties, so she was old. No one knew of any health problems, but one morning she went in to wake Ory and the little girl was dead. It literally drove the Mama crazy. She would stop people on the street and ask, 'Did you know that God took my little Ory as his newest angel?' A sad story for sure."

"We'll come again sometime and visit more graves and let you hear their stories too. Right now I want to do a little clean up and put some flowers on a couple of the graves. Why don't you just sit on the bench for awhile?"

I walked around and took a look at several more graves and then went to the bench. A little sun was hitting on it so it was very pleasant. I layed down and put my feet up on the end.

I was woken up by someone saying, "So you're the one they call Rabbit? I want to ask you one thing. Are you watching out for your grandma?"

I looked up to an old man. He had on an old-timey suit. The strangest thing was his right sleeve was empty. There was no arm in it. It was just pinned up to his suit jacket.

"I want to make sure you're taking care of her. She was always my favorite."

The next thing I remember was my grandma shaking my

arm. "Wake up Rabbit. It's time to go back to the house."

I bolted out of the bench.

"Grandma, your great uncle just talked to me. He wanted to know if I was watching out for you. The same question he asked Virge. Do you reckon I really saw a ghost?"

"Oh, most likely you just had a little dream."

"I don't know, it just seemed so real."

I couldn't wait to get back to the house so I could tell Virge I saw my great great-uncle too. I found Virge sitting on his front porch, reading the paper.

"Hey Virge, Grandma and I walked over to the cemetery. I'm pretty darn sure I talked to Robert White, cause this old man showed up and asked me the same thing he asked you, was I watching out for my grandma."

Virge dropped his paper and said, "For real?"

"You know I wouldn't make something like that up."

"What did he look like?"

"Well, he was an old man, dressed in an old-timey suit. He had long white hair with sideburns. His mustache was right long and drooped down on each side."

"Was there anythin' else kind of peculiar about him?"

I scrunched up a second then blurted out, "Yeah, he didn't have no right arm. The sleeve was just pulled back and pinned to his jacket."

I'm not sure I ever heard Virge cuss before, but he said, "Well I'll be damned!"

He smiled at me and went on. "Mister Robert got shot in the right arm during the civil war. He got the gangrene and they had to cut it off. See Rabbit, I ain't crazy after all."

Chapter 16

Going Home

I watched a movie with my grandma and grandpa about a cowboy about to be hanged. News to me, but it appears that the prisoner gets to choose their last meal. This guy had country fried steak, potatoes, gravy, biscuits and green beans. That was the way that I felt this morning. Not that I was a prisoner, but my summer stay was ending. Late morning, my dad was picking me up to take me home to Alabama. Of course, my grandma's breakfast was everything I loved. She had eggs, country ham with red-eye gravy, grits, biscuits and sliced, fresh tomatoes. I couldn't help but think of that movie. It seemed like a last meal.

My grandma was kind of teary eyed. "Rabbit, you don't need to do any gardening work this morning. If you don't mind, just bring in the eggs. Then, you ought to go and say goodbye to Virge."

I suppose that some folks might think it strange, being that Virge was ninety years old and black, but was my best friend. To be honest, best friend don't really describe things. I loved that old man. Part of me wanted to just sneak home and not see him again. It was going to hurt so bad to say goodbye.

After gathering the eggs, I trudged up through the pastures to Virge's cabin. As I got near, I saw that he wasn't on his front porch. He was home though, because I could smell his Sir Walter Raleigh pipe smoke. It smells like sweet smoke and cherries. He and my grandpa both smoked the same brand.

Walking around the back side of his cabin, I spotted him.

As I approached, Virge gave me the shush sign and waved me forward. Going up to the back porch, it appeared that he was intently staring at the space next to his house. "Come here, Rabbit, and take a look at this."

What he was watching was his kitten, Buttons, stalking something in the weeds. I slid up next to him and asked, "What are you looking at?"

"Well Rabbit, this here is just fascinating. I know you got television and stuff, but entertainment don't get no better than this."

"What are you talking about?"

"Just look at Buttons. He's been a house-kitty all his life. If he wasn't feeding off his mamma's teat, he was getting food from me. But look at him. He's stalking our snake, Slick, who came out from under the house. It's like he's a wild tiger or something. See how Buttons is creeping up, hiding behind tufts of grass?"

"I see him, but I don't get it."

"The point is, he ain't never been trained to hunt. He's just doing it naturally. Not only that, but look at old Slick. He's agitating his tail among all them leaves so they rattle like a rattlesnake. Now that's not something he read in a book. He just does that naturally too. Do you know why?"

"No, I guess I don't."

"Well, it's called instinct. They don't have to learn it, they's just born with it. There are other types of learning. Do you remember when you used to get Skippy's leash out?"

"Yes, I do. He would start doing his dance, because he knew we would take a walk."

"That's right, Rabbit. Old Skippy had learned that when you pulled that leash out he expected to go for a walk. He put those two things together in his mind, Leash means walk. That there is called conditional learning."

"Virge, how do you know all this stuff?"

"Your grandma brings me all those National Geographic Magazines. I read them, the Atlanta Journal, the LaGrange Daily News and the Bible. Between the four, there are all sorts of things to learn."

"I reckon you get another use for those newspapers, since there's always a stack of them in your outhouse. I'm kind of partial to the funny papers. The magazines come from my house in Alabama. I never read them. I do look at the pictures."

"Well, you goin' home today and I want you to promise that you are going to start readin' them. That way, when you come back, we'll have all sorts of things to talk about. Let's go inside and get some iced tea."

We walked into Virge's cabin. He had an old icebox. Pulling out a hunk of ice, he put it into his wooden ice bucket and whacked it into chunks with an ice pick. He then filled two mason jars with ice and tea. We didn't have any lemon, but he did put mint in from his yard and some berries from a sumac tree. If I hadn't seen the berries, I would have sworn it was lemon. I don't know why, but that chopped up ice always seemed to make the tea taste better. We walked out to the front porch and got in two rockers. The front porch was always in the shade, and generally there was a nice breeze.

For awhile, we just rocked.

Finally, Virge said, "I am glad you come by. I know this is your last day here this summer. I want you to know that havin' you at your grandma's made my summer a heap better. We had us some good times."

"We sure did. I do want to get home, but I'm going to miss being here on the farm."

We rocked some more before Virge said, "How about one more game of checkers?"

Checkers was something that Virge taught me at the beginning of the summer. We played almost every day. I hadn't won yet, but was getting better.

"I'd like that game of checkers. I reckon it's just about time I won a game."

Virge pulled a small barrel between our chairs. The checker board was already there, so it looked like he was ready for a game. I tried all the tricks he taught me over the summer and was doing pretty darned good. For awhile, I thought maybe Virge was letting me win. I took a peek at him though and suspect that he wasn't. His eyes were scrunched up more than usual. It looked like his wrinkles had wrinkles. He was trying hard.

Right when I thought I had him, Virge made me jump into a sucker play. He wound up getting one of my kings and two other checkers. It was all over. Pushing the barrel aside, Virge said, "Rabbit, you done real good. I've been playing checkers all my life and you durn near beat me. I compliment you on your play and also your ways. Your brother JJ gets madder than a wet hen when he loses."

"Well, it may not have been in that National Geographic about learnin', but there was something that you taught me earlier in the summer."

"What was that, Rabbit?"

"You taught me that if you try your best and things don't work out, just walk away with your head high and a smile on your face. I tried my best and almost beat you. Maybe next time I will. Anyhow, I'd better be getting back to the house. My dad will be there soon to pick me up."

As I got ready to leave, Virge said, "Now wait just a minute, Rabbit. Ain't you going to give old Virge a hug?"

Smiling at Virge, I said, "Guys don't hug. What if we just shake hands?"

He stuck his hand out and I reached out to shake. Of course, he tricked me, grabbed my hand and pulled me into a hug. I didn't struggle, just hugged him back. He's an old man and don't get too many hugs.

As I left and got near the side of his yard, I turned around and hollered, "Virge, do you keep your Sir Walter Raleigh in a can?"

With a puzzled look, he replied, "I sure do, why?"

"Well, it's about time you let his ass out!" I turned and ran toward the house. I didn't turn back and look, but I could hear his deep, from the gut, laughter.

There were tears in my eyes.

Chapter 17

Dinosaurs

When Dad came to pick me up, he already had JJ in the back seat. His greeting to me so typical, "Hey Punk."

"All right, you two, we haven't even started the trip back to Alabama. Let's try and be pleasant."

When we drove away from Grandma's, we had to go by Virge's cabin. I didn't see Virge, but asked Dad to honk anyhow. He did. To me it seemed like we had just made this trip in reverse. Hard to believe that we came down in early June and now August was ending in one day. *What happened to the summer?*

Within five minutes JJ and I were fussing in the back seat. Dad turned back and asked, "What's wrong?"

"Rabbit's bothering me."

"What's he doing?"

"He's breathing."

"My God, boys, I know why your mom had you two out of the house and separated. Maybe we need to play the animal count game."

The animal count game was a simple game. Each player picked one side of the car. You counted the number of four legged animals that you saw. If a church with a cemetery came by, you had to 'bury' your animals and start over from zero. The game was kind of cool on a new road, but we had traveled from LaGrange, Georgia to Eufaula, Alabama a million times.

The person on the driver's side, (JJ) was going to win every time. Of course, JJ was all for it.

Dad added a wrinkle. "I know we've been this way a lot of times, so here is a new wrinkle. If there is even one single car in the parking lot, you get a free pass. That should make it more interesting."

I liked this added rule. JJ probably didn't think on it, but I remembered that the last church and cemetery that we passed was a single car Catholic church. I read the signs outside and knew that they had a service every Saturday as well as on Sunday. We'd go by a little early for their Saturday service, but I figured somebody would be there. I also knew that there was a large dairy farm right before the church on JJ's side. There were always cows and calves all over the place. I could feel it coming on. *I was going to kick JJ's ass.*

JJ was racking up pretty good. There is a large farm about two miles from the turn-off to Grandma's house. His side of course. So far, I had two dogs and JJ had two mules and nine cows. Eleven to two against me and we'd just started. He racked up even more when we passed a horse farm. All of a sudden, the score was eighteen for JJ and only five for me. Of course, we knew a church with cemetery was coming up. It was the church that Grandma and Grandpa go to. We passed it, and no cars in the lot! Just like that, my brother is back to zero.

Dad's new rule did make the game more exciting. I reckon it's just Georgia and Alabama, but you can't go too far without passing a church with a cemetery. The lead seemed to pass back and forth pretty often. About half way home, I got lucky with lots of animals to count and I got a free pass at one of the churches on my side. All of a sudden, the score is thirty-two for me and zero for JJ.

We passed a chicken farm on JJ's side, and he piped up, "I believe there must be at least seventy for my side."

"What do you mean seventy? We're counting four legged animals, not two. That's a bunch of bull crap!"

"Now, Rabbit, you know your mom and I don't like you boys using language like that. JJ, you do know that we only count four legged animals."

I looked at JJ and stuck my tongue out, but he ain't never been short for words.

"All right Mister Smarty, let me ask you a question. If we came across a dinosaur on my side, would you let me count that?"

I had no idea where he was going with this, but had to answer, "Yeah, I reckon so."

"You spent the whole summer not learning a thing. You just hung out with your old black friend and fished and stuff."

"Yeah, and so?"

"I was learning the whole summer. Grandma Nan, got the whole new set of Encyclopedia Britannica and I read the whole series from A to Z. One of the things I learned was birds are descended from dinosaurs. Their wings ain't nothing more that what's called a 'prehensile' arm. So, if you would let me count a dinosaur, you should let me count chickens."

My dad responded to this one. "JJ that *is* a bunch of bull crap. We are not going to allow chickens."

The game went on for the rest of the trip. My memory of the Catholic Church was right. The large dairy farm and then lots of cars in the lot made me the big winner.

Dad drove up to our house in Eufaula. "Okay, boys, welcome home."

This *was* my home and I'd soon seen my mom, my new sister and Bubba. I was happy, but also sad. I already missed the farm and my buddy Virge. I quickly wiped a tear from my cheek.

Chapter 18

A Righteous Whipping

Mama said it was the *Three Little Bears* time of year. It wasn't too hot, it wasn't too cold, it was just right. Late October in Eufuala, Alabama, was pretty durn good. We could have some surprises, but me and my brothers were mostly still wearing shorts. I suppose our lives were pretty much okay. My sister was three months old and didn't look like a frog anymore.

My mother and her twin sister planned on driving down to Florida to show off the new baby to relatives. My dad was in the military, stationed at a radar station in Eufaula, Alabama. I don't know much, but that radar was pointed toward Cuba, and my dad couldn't leave.

With them going, a question would be who would watch my brothers and me during the day. It would be fine with my dad, but he just couldn't do it. We had to stay in school, so needed to stay in Eufuala.

Mom explained the situation. “I've asked Miss Carrie to come over and stay with you. Y'all know her. She's a great cook and knows you and all our family. I know you'll be just fine. It's only going to be five days. I expect all of you to behave at your very best. Please, please, be good, and I'll be home soon.”

My brothers and I promised to be good.

I'm only nine years old, so don't know a whole lot of people. Miss Carrie, I know real well. She's Virge's niece. He seems to have a nick-name for everybody. Her's was Sugar Butts.

Mom's news to me was great. I was anxious to be able to talk to Miss Carrie and catch up what was going on with Virge. Other than summer months, we usually go to my grandparents, once or twice a month. With the new baby, we hadn't been one single time since late August. She'll be able to tell me what all's been happening on the farm and what Virge is up to.

Miss Carrie arrived on the Greyhound bus. It was a great day, lots of sun and just a few stringy clouds. She got off the bus wearing her Sunday best, a colorful print cotton dress, a little straw hat with plastic flowers and carrying a big hop-sack cloth purse. She greeted us with a smile that reminded me of Virge. It was one of those ear to ear white tooth smiles that made you smile right back.

We all got a big hug and she said, “Jackie, I'm going to take care of y'all like you're my own family.” She and my grandma were the only people I knew who called my dad, Jackie.

It didn't take long for things to develop into a rhythm. Miss Carrie's cooking was as good as ever. It was built around fried meats, but to us, wonderful. She even introduced us to some vegetables not seen around our house. Smashed rutabagas and turnips, with butter and cinnamon became a favorite. No meal was complete without biscuits or cornbread. A change for us, she mostly fried the cornbread in little pancake size pieces. After brown bagging lunch for years with bologna or peanut butter and jelly sandwiches, my bag was now full of stuff like fried salmon patties or hunks of ham tucked into biscuits.

After one day, us boys got back to normal—stinkers. Bubba was a good boy and rarely did anything wrong. For some reason, I picked on him constantly. My dad once asked why I did it. I had to shrug my shoulders and say, "I dunno'." It might have to do with the fact that JJ picked on me. Virge once explained it as, "Turds roll down hill." For now, Bubba was at the bottom of the hill.

My torment this day was to hand him his favorite toy and at the last second, jerk it back and say, "No. it's mine." He started crying.

Carrie walked into the living room and hollered at me, "Rabbit, what are you doing to make Bubba cry?"

"Nothin'"

"Well, whatever nothin' you doin', it best stop or I'll give you a whuppin!"

Looking right at Miss Carrie, I said a couple of things that came back to haunt me.

"Sugar Butts, you can't whip me!"

Looking up over her glasses and giving me the evil eye, she asked, "And why can't I whup you?"

"Cuz you're a nigger." I could see the change on her face.

She proved me wrong on the whipping. Out of nowhere she got a fly swatter and started wailing away at my back side. Fly swatters must be the perfect thing for whipping. You get the switching, but you also get the sound. *Swisssh, pop, swisssh, pop, swisssh, pop*. She got me good.

"See there, smarty pants, I can whup you."

Rubbing my butt, I told her right quick, "When my daddy gets home I'm going to tell on you."

All that working caused her glasses to slide down lower on her nose. Looking over at them, she snapped, "If you're smart, you won't tell your daddy. This can just be between the two of us."

"Nope, I'm going to tell him the minute he walks

through the door. You just watch me."

"Okay, tell him if you want, but it ain't real smart."

When Dad walked through the door, I almost attacked him. "Miss Carrie whipped me this afternoon."

Looking at Carrie, he asked, "Why did you whip him?"

She let me off easy by saying, "He was tormentin' little Bubba so bad, he was cryin' his head off."

"Uh-huh, what did you whip him with?"

"I popped him with the flyswatter."

"Hand it to me."

I just knew Dad was going to whip Miss Carrie. *Swisssh, pop, swisssh, pop, swisssh, pop.* It was my butt!

After he was done, he crossed the kitchen to the refrigerator, pulled out a Falstaff and headed to his favorite chair to read the paper.

Miss Carrie took a look at me and said, "You about the smartest little boy that I know, but sometimes, you just plain dumb. When your daddy was about your age, your grandma had to work at the cotton mill for a spell. I took care of your daddy every day. He and my boy, Joe, got into all sorts of mischief. Your grandma told me to whup your daddy if he needed it, but to tell her when she got home, so she could whup him too."

"So, you knew he was going to whip me?"

"Yep, I did. I warned you, but you just had to blab. I could have told your daddy what you said, and I bet your whuppin' would have been worse. What you said needs to stay between you and me. You ought not to call me Sugar Butts. I know my old fool Uncle says it, but you best not. I know what I look like and it don't help to have a smart ass little boy call me that. Lots of people in my life have called me nigger." her chin quivered, "But nobody I loved. Most people who use that word are just ignorant and I know you're not. You know it would hurt me. Why would you say it to me?"

That flyswatter didn't make me cry at all. This made my eyes drip. She was right. I know she loved me and I loved her too. My answer was one I used way too much, "I dunno'." After a snuffle and wiping my nose across my sleeve, I asked, "Do you remember when you and Virge took me to that revival at your church?"

"I do remember. That's the one where Reverend Jimmy from Atlanta did the preachin'."

"Yes ma'am, that's the one. When he was preachin' he turned around and pointed his finger right at me and hollered, *Do you want to go to heaven*? It was kind of warm that day and I was leaning against you and restin' my eyes. That woke me up and I hollered right back, Yes, I do. Everybody in church said amen."

Miss Carrie chuckled a little and said, "I do remember, but I don't think he was pointin' and talkin' just to you. He meant it for all of us."

"I dunno' he looked right at me. He also said the road to Heaven was a rough and rocky one, because as good as you are, if you ain't careful you'll start listening to the devil. The only thing I can figure is maybe I said those things because the devil made me do it. Do you reckon that's possible?"

"I don't know, maybe. All I know is that you said them. For me, it's in the past and I'm going to forget them. I would like for you to remember one thing. As you go through life, don't speak to nobody in a mean way. I'm pretty sure I'm going to heaven and would like to think that you'll be there too. Will you promise to do what I asked?"

"I do promise Miss Carrie, unless...."

"Unless what?"

"Unless the devil makes me do it."

Chapter 19

Last Visit

When you're used to getting up in the morning to the sound of a rooster crowing, it's tough to just get on up without it. Now that I 'm home in Alabama, the new day is announced by my father yelling up the stairs, "Awake, awake, the dawn is here, the air is full of atmosphere."

I wish he'd just say, "Cockle-Doodle-Doo."

Not a day goes by when I don't miss the farm in Georgia. I bet I've asked myself a million times, "I wonder what Virge is doing?" We used to visit my grandma's pretty often as it's only a ninety-minute trip, but with my new baby sister, mama doesn't want to travel. My dad says maybe we'll go for Thanksgiving.

When I first saw my sister's picture, I thought she looked like a frog, but now I think she's pretty cute. She likes me more than my two brothers. She must be smart. I don't have chickens and a garden to take care of, but helping take care of my sister, Carolyn, is fun. My mom actually gave me a big hug the other day, because I changed Carolyn's diapers. She said, "You're one up on your brothers and tied with your dad."

"Mama, there are a lot of things in life worse than baby poop. I shoveled and moved around worse stuff all summer." That got me another hug.

Life was back to normal. School seemed even more fun than last year. Bobbie Joe Herlong told me she wanted to be my girlfriend. Funny though, she said, "I don't want to call you Rabbit. It sounds baby-like. Can I call you Billy?"

I smiled, batted my eyes, and said, "You can call me anything you want."

When my dad came home from work, I don't think I've ever seen a longer face. He doesn't hug much, but he asked me to come over to where he was sitting. He gave me a hug before saying, "Rabbit, I'm sorry I've got to bring you some bad news. Our good friend Virge is dead."

School was in session, so my parents decided mom would stay home with the baby and my two brothers. Dad and I would go to Georgia for the funeral. Mom had to give me JJ's 'go-to-stuff-suit'. I had outgrown mine. We packed up and headed to Georgia.

Traveling down the road, we kept our thoughts to ourselves. I finally asked my dad, "What did Virge die from?"

"Well, Son, you'd think Virge just died of old age. He just turned ninety-one, but that wasn't what caused his death. The old coot climbed up on top of his roof to sweep some leaves off. He fell and broke some ribs. They got him to the hospital and patched him up. Everybody thought he was going to be okay, but he developed pneumonia in his lungs and died. At least Carrie and Joe Leslie were with him. Carrie was the one who called me."

"I wish I had been there. I'd have climbed the roof and....and....knocked those leaves off for him."

"I know you would have. We just have to accept it was his time. I've known Virge my entire life and have to admit things won't seem the same without him. I was thinking last night of the last time I saw him this summer. He didn't look any different to me than he did when I was your age. He's been old forever. He's had a pretty good ride."

The trip to LaGrange was a quiet one. When we pulled

onto the dirt road to my grandparents' house, we drove right by Virge's cabin. It was the first time I cried. I wiped my eyes and looked at my dad. His eyes were red and puffy too.

I got out and opened the gate in front of the house. Grandma came out of the house to greet us. Without saying a word, she gathered me in her arms and gave me a big hug. She stepped back and I could see tears in her eyes. She finally said, "I'm sure glad to see my two boys though I'm sorry it is under such sad circumstances. Y'all come up and sit on the front porch. I'll bring you some iced tea." Even though it was early November, it still was pleasant outside.

We sat there for a while, rocked, drank some iced tea, and took turns telling Virge stories. They laughed like crazy when I told them about the yellow jacket war. Grandpa finally got home from work. We all went in to dinner. It was strange, because it was left-overs. There were collards from the garden in the sink and a bunch of pork chops soaking in brine. I asked Grandma if we were going to have them for dinner. She smiled and touched my face before replying, "No, honey, I'm going to fry up those pork chops and fix the collards tomorrow morning. You and your daddy are going to bring them by Virge's church tomorrow. They're going to have some food after the service."

"You could bring it. Ain't you and Grandpa goin'?"

She brushed some strands of hair away from her face before replying, "No, Rabbit, Grandpa and I won't be going tomorrow."

It took me a few moments to reply because I was confused. "Grandma, Virge has been around you since you were a little girl. How come you ain't goin' to the church?"

"Honey, your grandpa and I have never been to a Negro church. It just wouldn't be right."

I started to say something, but my dad pinched my leg beneath the table. I just shrugged and shut up. Later, I was even more confused when I found out my grandparents paid for Virge's hospital stay and for his funeral. I don't know. There's just a lot of stuff I don't understand.

Dad and I got to the church early. Some of the people came by to speak to him, but more came my way. I don't think Dad knew I'd been to Virge's church about six or seven times over the summer. Even the preacher from Atlanta came over. He shook my hand and said, "I remember you. You're Rabbit, the young man who professed to the congregation you wanted to go to heaven. Just know old Virge will be there before you. He'll be waiting."

"Yes Sir, I reckon he will be, and I'll be glad to see him. I've got to tell you though, I ain't in no hurry."

He laughed and said, "Indeed, young man, indeed."

My dad introduced himself. When the preacher left, Dad turned to me and winked. "Son, you never cease to amaze me."

Before the service, we were sitting down near the back. Miss Carrie had tried to get us to sit with family, but my dad said, "Son, we should just sit in the back." He leaned over and whispered to me, "Son, it's an open casket. Do you want to go up and see Virge one last time?"

I blinked back a tear before saying, "No, Sir, I don't need to. That's not Virge up there in that box. He's dead and his soul is in heaven. It's like when you shell purple hull peas. When you're done, you've got a big pile of hulls. They ain't peas no more. If I want to see Virge, all I have to do is close my eyes."

My dad pulled his handkerchief out and wiped the front of his face. I reckon he was hot.

In a few minutes, my favorite time at Virge's church started. The back doors opened and the choir came in. They don't walk in, they dance in. They move with the music, clapping their hands and swaying side to side. They were singing one of Virge's favorite songs, 'His Eye is on the Sparrow'. I remember sitting on his front porch and him playing the song on his harmonica. If Miss Carrie was there she would sing. I don't remember all of it, but remember this part: "I sing because I'm happy, I sing because I'm free, For His eye is on the sparrow, and I know He watches me."

It was a great service. Lots of people went up front and told stories about Virge. I knew him about as well as anyone, but learned all sorts of stuff I didn't know. It seemed strange to me to find out that Virge learned to read and write when he was sixty years old. I thought you started reading early in school. The person telling this story was Miss Carrie's son, Joe Leslie. He gestured to the congregation and acknowledged my father, saying, "It was Mr. Jack and me who taught him. We would learn in school and come home and teach Virge. It didn't take him long to start helping us."

After the service, I was standing around a picnic table set up outside. I was picking out fried chicken wings. Even then, I thought about Virge. He would have been picking out chicken livers. I looked up as Virge's niece, Miss Carrie, walked over. I greeted her with a big old smile, which she returned. Part of the smile was joy in seeing her. Another reason I smiled is on my last day with Virge he asked me to not just look at the pictures, but read the National Geographic Magazines my mom gave him. I now loved reading them. I wanted to tell Virge I read a story about some tribes in Africa. It was natural for some black women to have big butts. I wanted to tell him it was in their genes and was thought a thing of beauty. Apparently, it went way back. In times when people were real hungry and thirsty, having a big butt kept some folks alive. I reckon if hard times come, Miss Carrie and my cousin Wesley will outlive us all.

When Miss Carrie got there, she gave me a huge hug

and said, "I sure am glad you and your daddy could come. Virge would have liked that. I got sumpin' for you." She handed me a box, wrapped in some 'Atlanta Journal' comic pages and tied with twine. “We're all dyin' to know what's inside, so why don't you open it.”

As my usual practice, I tore into the box. The first thing I saw was a hand-written note from Virge. It read, “Hey Rabbit—I guess you know I'm dead. Remember the first time we went fishin'? You was worried about them worms eatin' cow poop and through nature gettin' into Grandma's tomatoes. It's time for them worms to get to Virge. Don't you worry though. They're plantin' me a long way from those tomatoes. HA HA! I don't want you to be sad today. Just think about ol Virge with a smile. We had us some good times.”

Beneath the note were some other things; a checker board, a small paper sack of checker pieces, his Barlow knife and a Sir Walter Raleigh tobacco tin. I picked up the tin and it rattled. Inside was a note saying, “I let his ass out.” Also inside were two arrowheads and a silver dollar. The date on the dollar was 1869, the year Virge was born.

I closed my eyes. Virge ain't dead to me.

He never will be.

William Hogg

About the Author

William Hogg

Bill has authored several short stories and is active on a blog site. This is his first novel. He lives with his wife in a town that *Southern Living* just named the greatest small town in Alabama, Fairhope.

Made in USA - North Chelmsford, MA
1306442_9781945190353
02.23.2022 1620